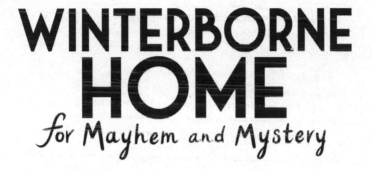

WINTERBORNE
HOME
for Mayhem and Mystery

ALSO BY ALLY CARTER

Winterborne Home for Vengeance and Valor

WINTERBORNE HOME

for Mayhem and Mystery

ALLY CARTER

HOUGHTON MIFFLIN HARCOURT

Boston   New York

hmhbooks.com

The text was set in Bembo Book.

Cover and interior design by Kaitlin Yang

Library of Congress Cataloging-in-Publication Data is available.

ISBN 978-0-358-00440-0

Manufactured in the United States of America

DOC 10 9 8 7 6 5 4 3 2 1

4500817897

For Rose, Rachel, Carrie, and Sarah.
I couldn't have done it without you.

PROLOGUE

Everybody knew about the Sentinel.

That he wasn't real. That he didn't exist. That the masked man with the swords and the hat was nothing more than a ghost story made of shadow and mystery, legend and myth—a tale told to make children behave and villains beware.

Nobody knew the truth.

ONE

April had never been a normal girl. It wasn't like that made her special. At all. Seriously. There wasn't anything special about not having parents or a last name or a birthday — even a really anticlimactic birthday like Christmas or the Fourth of July. No. April wasn't *special,* you see. She was simply *not normal.*

After all, you can't possibly be normal when you don't have any money, but you also live in a mansion. When you don't have a family, but you're part of the Winterbornes. And, most of all, it's totally, absolutely, completely impossible to be normal when your roommate is Sadie Marie Simmons, inventor extraordinaire.

"Are you ready?" Sadie asked in a way that April had come to dread. Because Sadie had the *Sadie gleam* in her eyes and her hands were practically vibrating with glee and anticipation.

So April's hands started vibrating too. Just for completely opposite reasons. Her voice even cracked a little when she said, "Maybe we should wait on . . . someone."

But there was no one to wait *on,* and that was something even April didn't dare to mention.

"Gabriel's going to love this," Sadie told her. "You'll see. It's going to be such a big help until Smithers comes back. Or Ms. Nelson."

She looked sheepish at that last part, and April couldn't blame her. After all, Smithers had been gone for four weeks. First, to the International Association of Butlers convention, where he'd won the annual—and hotly contested—Buttle-Off (which was a good thing). But the grand prize was a cruise around the world (which was a bad thing). When he called to tell them the news, he swore he'd be home as soon as possible.

But Gabriel . . . Gabriel just swore.

April strongly suspected that had less to do with Smithers's extended absence and more to do with the fact that it had been three months since Isabella Nelson had fallen into the sea. Sure, Izzy had sent a note, telling them she was alive and well. But she hadn't come home. And now she'd been gone for twelve weeks. Eighty-four days. Not that April had been counting. (But April had totally been counting.)

Every day, the residents of Winterborne House woke up and hoped she'd be there, telling the kids to stop running on the stairs and Gabriel to shave and tuck his shirt in. But it was starting to look like Isabella Nelson might be gone for good.

Which was almost as scary as the look in Sadie's eye when she said, "Okay! Goggles ready?"

April didn't answer. She just grabbed the plastic safety goggles that Smithers bought in bulk and were a standard part of the Sadie Marie Simmons Friendship Package.

No sooner were April's goggles in place than Sadie was saying, "Now!"

Then she pulled a cord. A moment later, Smithers's big, fancy stove sprang to life. Flames sparked underneath a heavy cast iron griddle, and a mixer turned on and started stirring batter in a giant bowl. It all seemed harmless enough until the bowl began to slide down a track.

And slowly.

Began.

To.

Tip.

No! April wanted to cry, but the bowl couldn't have been more stable as it dripped batter onto the hot griddle in perfect little puddles of future pancakes.

"Wait for it . . ." Sadie said a few moments later, and April remembered to be scared. "Now!" Sadie exclaimed just as the piping-hot griddle popped up. The pancakes flipped. And every last one of them landed back on the griddle, perfect as you please.

"It worked," April said, equal parts stunned and relieved.

"Of course it worked." Sadie wasn't mad, and she wasn't defensive. It was just a data point in a long line of data points—every one of which said that the newest SadieMatic was ready for business.

April's heart rate was just starting to return to normal when Sadie grabbed a knife and said, "Now it's time to try bacon!"

But before April could even start to panic, someone said, "I'll do that, Sade!" and Tim swept into the kitchen. He snatched the sharp knife out of Sadie's hand before she could attach it to the SadieMatic Twenty, because it was the unwritten rule of Winterborne House that SadieMatics and knives should never, ever mix.

A moment later Tim had the bacon open and a second pan was sizzling on the stove and the whole room smelled like the best thing ever: breakfast. *Seriously,* April thought. *I ought to make a perfume that smells like breakfast.* She'd be richer than Gabriel if she did.

But that just made April think about Gabriel. Which made her glance at the clock: ten a.m.

Mornings were coming later and nights were lasting longer, and April had to wonder if it was the time of year or something else that was keeping Winterborne House more and more in the dark.

"Is he up?" April asked, but Tim just looked at her.

"I thought he was down here."

"I haven't seen him," she said, and they both glanced at Sadie, who beamed.

"I'll get him!" Then she ran to a small panel on the wall that had about a million buttons. They were old and brass, and had no doubt hung there, unused, for decades, but Sadie had recently made it her life's mission to resurrect the old intercom, and when she pushed the button, there wasn't even a hint of static as she said, "Gabriel! Kitchen to Gabriel's room. Gabriel, are you there?"

"He's not gonna answer if he's in a mood, Sade," Tim told her.

But that just made Sadie hold the button down a little more forcefully and yell a little louder, "Gabriel! Gabriel! Gabriel! Gab—" Then Sadie stopped abruptly and looked at Tim and April. "What if he's not ignoring me? What if he's gone?"

Tim glanced at April, then back at Sadie. "What do you mean, *gone?*"

"What if he's not in his room because he's . . . you know . . . out there." Sadie jerked her head toward the windows. "What if he's . . ." She dropped her voice. "*Sentineling?* What if he *Sentineled?*" she tried, but that didn't sound right either, so eventually she just snapped, "What if he *did it?*"

"I don't think so, Sade," Tim said.

"Why not?" Sadie said. "I mean . . . yeah. Sure. I always thought the Sentinel was an urban legend too, but now we know it's real! Think about it. The Sentinel has always been real! And it's always been a Winterborne. And

Gabriel is the only Winterborne left," Sadie said, as if two plus two always equaled masked vigilante. "Plus, Gabriel was already kinda superhero-y with his swords and stuff. It's his family legacy! Why couldn't he have slipped away last night and Sentineled?"

It seemed a perfectly logical question to Sadie, but April couldn't help but think about the answers. *Because he doesn't care about his family legacy? Because he's still not up to full strength after almost dying a few times, thanks to me? Because his body can't possibly be well—not while his heart is so totally broken?*

But instead, April said, "Because he would have told us, right?"

She looked at Tim, who must have read her mind because he shrugged and mumbled, "Sure."

And Sadie believed him. Because that's what Sadie did. "Yeah. That makes sense." She nodded sagely. "I'm getting really close to a prototype for his costume. He wouldn't want to go out without it. Which reminds me, should we stick with black? I know that's what the Sentinel ensemble has always been, but I've got to say, silver really brings out his eyes."

April knew she was serious because Sadie never, ever kidded about prototypes, but she didn't have a clue what to say. Luckily, she didn't have to say a thing because, just then, the kitchen door swung open and someone yelled, "Help!"

It sounded like Violet. It even looked like Violet. Or, well, it looked like *part* of Violet. Thin arms were sticking out of the top of a plaid jumper, flailing and fighting to either pull the jumper on or take it off. It was stuck in that very awkward in-between phase, and now Violet was trapped and blind and growing more desperate by the second.

"Get it off! Get it off! Get it —"

Rip.

At first, April thought the seam had given out, but then she saw Tim. And the knife. Slowly, Violet's head peeked out. Her short black hair was standing straight on end from all the static, and tears filled her eyes.

"It shrunk," she said.

"You grew," Tim corrected her, and he was right. Violet's jumpers had been getting shorter and shorter for weeks, and somehow, overnight, her clothes had gone from slightly snug to totally too small.

Her skirt was three inches too short. The sleeves of her white blouse were up almost to her elbows, and even with the giant slit in the back, she couldn't really move her arms very well. She'd grown so much since she came to Winterborne House that April might not have recognized the shy, timid, terrified girl she'd met not that long ago, except that her big brown eyes looked exactly the same.

"Ooh. Pancakes!" Instantly, Violet stopped crying and reached for the plate by the stove. "And bacon!" Violet piled a piece of bacon on top of a pancake, then rolled it up like a burrito, and April thought, *Violet is a breakfast prodigy!* But then a loud ripping sound filled the air again, and when Violet turned around, April could see the slice in her jumper had become a full-fledged tear going all the way down her back.

"Is Gabriel gonna be mad?" Violet whispered, and April didn't say what she was thinking: that Gabriel probably wouldn't even notice.

"Of course not," Sadie said. "It's not your fault you're growing. We'll order you some new ones, but in the meantime you can wear one of mine."

Sadie turned and darted into the laundry room off the butler's pantry, but she ran back a split second later. Her hands were empty, but her eyes were wide.

"What is it?" Tim asked.

"I found Gabriel." Sadie threw open the door and there sat Gabriel Winterborne, billionaire, recluse, guardian, and would-be vigilante, asleep atop a pile of laundry.

"So . . . *not* superheroing last night, I guess?" April said as Sadie crept closer.

If it hadn't been for the subtle rise and fall of his chest, April might have thought he'd died there, under the weight of all those sheets and towels and socks. But it took more than clothes to kill Gabriel Winterborne. After all, his Uncle Evert had been trying since Gabriel was ten, and now Evert was in jail and Gabriel was safe and sound and maybe drooling just a little bit.

"Should we wake him up?" Sadie whispered as Gabriel mumbled and grumbled. His stomach even rumbled, and even though the laundry was soft and fluffy, he couldn't have been very comfortable, so April crept closer.

"Gabriel?" she whispered, but he only grumbled louder. "Gabriel, wake up." She reached out to shake him by the shoulder which, in hindsight, might have been a mistake.

Nope.

It was *definitely* a mistake, April realized as a big hand

shot out and grabbed her wrist. In the next moment, she was flying through the air, over Gabriel's shoulder, and landing on a pile of fluffy white towels.

When he made a low, feral sound and put a hand around her throat, he didn't look like one of the richest men in the world, and he didn't sound like the boy who had grown up in a mansion with butlers and tutors and governesses.

In moments like that, you couldn't help but remember that Gabriel Winterborne had spent ten years on the run—training and fighting and waiting for the day he could kill the man who had killed his entire family.

But that plan hadn't worked.

Thanks to April.

She heard Sadie yell his name, and saw Tim pound on his shoulders, but Gabriel was too strong and his hands were too big, and his blank gaze stayed trained on April, who tried to shout, but the words were more like a croak.

"Gabriel!" she said. "Gabriel, wake up." She couldn't breathe. She couldn't think. She could only whisper, "Please!"

Then Gabriel froze. He blinked. Slowly, he seemed to wake up—to remember. But April didn't know if that was better or worse until his hands unclenched and he looked at her like he was the one who was terrified.

"April?" he asked, sounding confused.

"Breakfast," she answered, because that made everything better.

TWO

CHEMISTRY LESSONS

Gabriel Winterborne's beard was a little too thick, and his hair was a little too long, and April had to marvel at how quickly he'd stopped pretending to be the slick, suave, powerful man the world wanted him to be and started being the grumpy, growly, grouchy man who really hated to shave.

Sometimes April couldn't believe it had only been four months since she'd first found him sneaking around in the dark and sharpening his swords, but looking at him that morning, she couldn't shake the feeling that a part of Gabriel was still hiding. Well, she told herself. At least they'd gotten him out of the cellar. And now he smelled like fabric softener, which was, overall, a vast improvement.

He stifled a yawn on his way to the coffee maker, and

when he found the canister empty, he said what April suspected was a Portuguese curse word and tossed the can in the garbage.

Then he got a good look at Violet in her too-small shirt and the jumper with the ragged rip down the back. "What are you wearing?"

"Jumper?" Violet said, like maybe it was supposed to be a trick question.

"What are you eating?" he asked.

She shoveled the last bite into her mouth and mumbled, "Pancakes. Are there any more?"

Tim slid one onto her plate and she dug in like there wasn't enough food in the world.

Gabriel cut his eyes at April, as if everything were her fault. "She's growing," April said. "It happens. And she needs new clothes."

"I know that," he said. "In fact . . ." He pushed aside a pile of dirty dishes and found a cardboard box. "Here."

At first, April looked down at it, almost afraid. But Sadie grabbed the box and ripped into it like it held the secret to life itself. Then she froze. She seemed confused as she pulled out something plaid. Yards and yards of plaid.

"What is all this?" Sadie said.

"Clothes," Gabriel told her.

"What kind of clothes?" Sadie sounded concerned.

"Uniforms," he said simply, but what Sadie pulled out of the box was approximately three times bigger than Violet.

"What size uniforms?" Sadie asked.

"It didn't ask for her size." Gabriel sounded grumpy. And defensive. "It asked how old she is, so I said fourteen."

"I'm eight," Violet said then pulled her new jumper on over her old clothes. The skirt fell to the floor. The straps drooped off her shoulders.

"I'm pretty sure that's a *size* fourteen," Sadie said.

Gabriel tilted his head, like if he looked at Violet from another angle, everything might be a perfect fit. "So you'll have room to grow into it."

Sadie was just opening her mouth to argue when the door opened one last time and in strode Colin. His black hair was slicked back, and his eyes were bright. Colin had always looked enough like a young Gabriel Winterborne that Colin's con artist mother had once tried to pass him off as Gabriel's son, but this morning Colin looked more like Gabriel Winterborne was *supposed* to look than even Gabriel himself.

"Mail's here." Colin tossed a handful of envelopes and flyers and magazines onto the top of a stack that had grown so tall it was teetering. April held her breath, waiting for it all to tip over, but the pile settled, steady for the time being.

Then April realized there was one piece of mail still in Colin's hand. A postcard.

"Where's this one from?" Tim asked.

"Dublin," Colin said.

"Postmark?" Sadie asked.

Colin checked the back of the card. "A week and a half ago."

But no one asked if there was a message. They certainly didn't inquire who it was from.

Violet just took the postcard from Colin and went to the fridge, tucked it in behind the other cards they'd gotten over the past few months, and carefully fanned them out until you could see the first letter of every city, and the unmistakable message:

STILL MAD.

But while everyone else was watching Violet, April was watching Gabriel, who was trying very hard to act like he wasn't watching or waiting or wishing for anything at all.

"It's been three months," Colin said, because, sometimes, Colin was the bravest.

"I am aware," Gabriel said.

"So?" April prompted because, sometimes, April was the dumbest.

"So what?" Gabriel asked.

"So what are we going to do about it?"

"Time doesn't need our permission, April. It passes whether we want it to or not."

"Yeah. Duh. But we can control *what we do about it*." April threw her hands out in a very Sadie-ish *ta-da,* but she wasn't a *ta-da* kind of person, no matter how hard she tried.

"You need to get her back," Violet said simply.

She was maybe the one person Gabriel couldn't — or wouldn't — shout at. So he looked down at her and said, "She'll come back when she's ready."

"Just out of curiosity." Colin leaned against the counter and crossed his arms. "When will that be?"

"Drink your milk," Gabriel snapped.

"We're out of milk," Sadie said simply. "I used the last of it for the pancakes. We're out of baking powder too."

"No we aren't." He turned back to the pantry and pulled out a container.

"That's baking soda," Sadie said.

"So? It's the same thing."

He tried to push the box in her direction, but Sadie shuddered then screamed, "*Baking soda and baking powder are two different things!* They are not a direct, one-to-one substitution! *It's chemistry!*" Because if there were two things Sadie didn't mess around with, they were chemistry and pancakes.

"It's fine, Sadie. That's what I used," Gabriel explained.

And then all of the kids got real quiet. "Used for what?" Sadie asked slowly, almost afraid of the answer.

"The cake," Gabriel said.

"What cake?" Sadie whispered just as the room began to fill with smoke.

Alarms began to blare.

What followed might have been chaos in a normal house with normal children, but the kids of Winterborne House were calm and focused as Colin shouted, "Fire positions!" and, instantly, everyone flew into action.

Violet threw open the back doors while Tim opened the windows. Colin grabbed a dishtowel and started fanning the smoke detector that was blaring so loudly that April thought her ears might bleed.

She wasn't sure if she should be grateful that they had their procedure so down pat or a little terrified that they'd had that much practice.

April was reaching for the oven door as Gabriel said, "Stand back," but it was too late. Thick smoke billowed out, and the inside of the oven looked like what would happen if you put a very small volcano inside an even smaller cake pan.

Sadie turned on a fan and started blowing the smoke toward the open doors and windows, but ruined bits of cake clung to the bottom of the oven. And the top. And the sides.

Gabriel reached in and grabbed the pan, but no sooner had he pulled it out than he swore and shouted and threw the hot pan into the sink.

"That towel is damp!" Sadie said, too late.

Red welts were already forming along Gabriel's palms where he'd been burned from the steam coming off the wet towel and the hot pan.

"First aid positions!" Colin shouted, and then took off for the butler's pantry and Smithers's first aid kit.

"Here. Run it under cool water."

"It's fine, April," Gabriel said.

"You've got to stop—"

"I said it's fine!" he snapped, then seemed to feel badly about it. He put his hand under the cool running water, but he didn't face her as he said, "Sorry." Then he glanced back at the mess the cake had made of the oven and the floor and the sink and said, "Put baking powder on the list."

When a weird buzzing sound filled the air, April's first thought was that it was some new alarm warning of some new disaster. Everyone looked at the oven and the smoke detector, the doors and the windows, but they didn't have a protocol for random buzzing and nobody knew their positions.

"What is that?" April said, but no one answered. For a moment, it really looked like no one even knew, but then Sadie bolted upright and exclaimed, "It's working!"

"What's working?" Colin, Tim, and April all asked, sounding more than a little bit leery.

"The doorbell!"

"We have a doorbell?" the three of them asked again.

In the days after Gabriel returned, people had knocked and called and visited and pried. Winterborne House had been a revolving door of attorneys and reporters, business acquaintances and socialites. Everyone wanted a piece of the long-lost Winterborne, so Gabriel locked the gates and unplugged the phones and, eventually, even Smithers went away, and no one had made it past the walls of Winterborne House since.

When the buzz came again, April said, "I'll get it." But as she headed down the hall and across the foyer, she couldn't help but wonder who it might possibly be. After all, Smithers was somewhere in the South Pacific, and Izzy wouldn't ring the bell.

Except . . . what if Izzy was ringing the bell? Maybe she forgot her key . . . Maybe she thought they might not want her back . . . Maybe . . . April really didn't want to get her hopes up, but hopes have a way of rising with or without your permission, so April held her breath and threw open the door.

And came face-to-face with a woman who absolutely, positively wasn't Isabella Nelson, and April felt almost sick with disappointment.

"Who're you?" April asked.

She was the kind of woman who didn't really have an

age. April suspected she'd always been old. And cranky. Her mouth looked like she'd put too much lemon in her water and then sucked a seed up the straw and she hadn't quite gotten around to spitting it out yet.

When the woman's lips parted, she said, "Who *are you?*" as if to show April how it should be done.

"I asked first," April said. "Besides, I didn't ring your doorbell, now, did I?"

This time, the woman looked like she'd been slapped, but April hadn't even taken her hand off the door.

"Where is your guardian?" the woman asked.

"I don't have one," April said, even though that wasn't strictly true. Izzy had headed up the Winterborne Foundation, and the foundation had established the home, and since Gabriel was technically the head of the foundation now, she supposed that made him her guardian. But, frankly, half the time April felt like *she* was responsible for *him*. And that was before he started falling asleep on piles of laundry. Really, he'd been way less worrisome when he'd been unconscious. And bleeding.

The woman considered April's words, then reached for a teeny-tiny pencil that hung from a silver chain around her neck. Like a whistle.

"I'm looking for Gabriel Winterborne," the woman clarified, and April had to laugh.

"Lady, you aren't the first." (She was, however, the oldest. But, wisely, April kept that part to herself.)

If possible, the pencil seemed even smaller when the woman started writing, whispering the words under her breath. "Lets children open doors to strangers." She glanced at April, then added, "Unsupervised!" and underlined the word twice for good measure.

"Look, he's eating breakfast," April said helpfully. "And he's grumpy. And we're out of coffee, so he's gonna get grumpier, but if you want to tell me what you—"

"April, get back here!" a deep voice shouted from the kitchen, and the woman took her tiny pencil and wrote, "Exhibits lack of anger management—"

"*Who are . . .*" April started, but she didn't finish. She didn't have to. Because April had spent ten long years going between group homes and foster homes and every kind of home that wasn't a home at all, and now a new kind of buzzing was filling April's head. This time, it wasn't smoke. And it wasn't the door. It was a warning of a completely different kind.

Then, for the first time, the woman smiled. It wasn't a

real smile, though. It was more like a smirk that said, *Gotcha.* She pulled a business card from her purse, shoved it in April's direction, and pushed into the house.

April didn't want to look down. She didn't want to read the words. In truth, she didn't even have to, but she did it anyway.

Gladys Pitts, case agent. Child Protective Services.

April had been out of the system too long. She was getting soft. And sloppy. And her social worker radar must have been way out of whack because the woman was inside and halfway down the hall before April had the sense to panic.

"Oh no. Ms. Pitts! Wait. Here. Hello. I'm April." April darted and jogged and tried to catch up, but the woman was too far down the corridor, halfway to the kitchen and . . . oh no. The screams.

"I like your tiny pencil!" April tried, running along in the woman's wake.

Sadly, the screams got louder.

"Why don't you wait here while I get Gab—I mean Mr. Winterborne. It's such a big house. He wouldn't want you to get lost. No. He'd want to see you in the . . . library.

Yeah. The library. I'll take you there and then I'll go find him and then—"

She didn't expect the woman to stop. And turn. And give April the smile that wasn't really a smile again.

"Oh, I think I can find him," the woman said, and pushed against the kitchen door, which swung open into a room that bore little resemblance to the kitchen April had left just minutes before.

For starters, the SadieMatic Twenty must have gone rogue, because the mixer was on and going fast. Too fast. Batter was flying around the room, flinging like shrapnel. A cloud of flour billowed up, filling the air, and April choked as it blew closer.

On the stove, bacon was starting to splatter. Violet was spinning in circles, still wearing a jumper that was at least five sizes too large for her. Pieces of ruined cake were all over the floor, and smoke still filled the air, and the whole room smelled like Breakfast Gone Terribly, Terribly Wrong.

And then the eggs started flying.

Gabriel was yelling at Sadie, and Sadie was yelling at Colin, and Tim was yelling, "Violet!" and pulling her out of the path of a rogue egg that was headed right for her head.

But, thanks to Tim's quick thinking, it missed Violet and kept flying. End over end. Like a small white missile, headed directly for—

Splat.

Finally, Gabriel reached the outlet and unplugged the SadieMatic. Tim turned off the stove, and the bacon stopped burning.

But the bits of eggshell still hung in the woman's hair.

Bright yellow yolk dripped down into her eyes.

And everyone stood, frozen, staring, as Violet said, "Put eggs on the list."

THREE

THE INSPECTION

April supposed, technically speaking, that it *could* have gone worse.

After all, there hadn't actually been a fire—just a minor cake explosion that didn't even make it out of the oven. Sure, every single person in Winterborne House (with the possible exception of April herself) looked like they'd been in a food fight. And the food had won. But no one was actually bleeding. Aside from Gabriel's hand, no one was even injured.

So for a moment she just stood there in the cold air that smelled like burned flour, waiting for something else to flip or fly or snap or catch fire. But once the smoke had (literally) cleared, she found a way to say, "Gabe . . .

er … Mr. Winterborne. We have company. This is Ms. Pitts."

"April—"

"She's from *Child Protective Services,*" April said pointedly. Really, she did everything but wink. But, mostly, she prayed that Gabriel would know what that meant.

He opened his mouth, but whether to argue or to growl April would never know because a pancake picked that moment to dislodge itself from the ceiling and fall onto the woman's head.

"Bad timing, that," Colin muttered, but otherwise, the room was utterly silent as everyone stood—not moving. Not speaking. Maybe not even breathing as they waited for what came next.

"Mr. Winterborne—" The woman's tone was cold and the words were crisp, but Gabriel didn't wait for her to finish

"My uncle was Mr. Winterborne, madam. He's in jail, if you haven't heard. But I'm here. Call me Gabriel."

Gabriel was young enough. And handsome enough. And, let's face it, *rich* enough, that it should have sounded roguishly charming. But while Gabriel had roguish down pat, charming was still a bit elusive.

The woman made the lemon face again and spoke slowly, "Mr. Winterborne. My name is Gladys Pitts. I am your new case agent."

Which wouldn't have been the worst sentence in the world except Gabriel turned to the kids and said, "We had an old case agent?"

Colin narrowed his eyes and shot Gabriel a you're-blowing-this expression, and Gabriel turned back to the woman.

"I mean yes. So nice to meet you, Ms. Pitts. Welcome to Winterborne House. Can I offer you a cup of coffee?"

"Coffee's on the list," Violet reminded him.

"Or tea," Gabriel said.

"Tea's on the —"

"How may I help you, Ms. Pitts?" Gabriel said like he was reading lines in a play he really didn't want to be in.

"Mr. Winterborne!" the woman began again. "Normally, I do not handle cases personally, but given the . . . shall we say . . . *notoriety,* and the . . ." She trailed off and looked around at the eggs, the flour, the bacon, and the pancake batter that was slowly dripping down the walls and off the ceiling. "Exceptional circumstances . . ."

"Did you hear that?" Colin gave a wry smile. "We're exceptional."

But the woman wasn't impressed.

"I see no choice but to take a personal interest in your situation. And, I must say, if this is the way you prepare for your inspection —"

"Inspection?" every resident of Winterborne House asked at once, but it was like the woman didn't even hear them.

"In twenty-three years, I have never worked with a guardian who refused to reply to a single letter . . ."

"There were letters?" Gabriel asked just as the massive pile of mail tipped and fell, cascading to the floor.

At which point the woman picked up her tiny pencil and began to write on her clipboard.

"Cleanliness of home environment . . ." She looked around and pursed her lips and made a note. "Nutritional needs of the children being met . . ." She turned and studied the rest of the kitchen, opening the massive (but mostly empty) refrigerator before making a check mark that April couldn't see but that sounded very judgmental. (Or as judgmental as a check mark could actually sound.)

That might have been the worst of it, but she eventually made her way to Violet, who was wearing a dress designed for a teenager — over a second dress that Tim had sliced open with a knife.

"Children's *physical* needs —"

"It's my fault!" Sadie finally exclaimed. "I made the SadieMatics! I'm Sadie," she added helpfully. "I make Sadie-Matics. They never work right until they do. The Sadie-Matic Nineteen just turned out *so well,* you know, that I felt like I was on a roll and so —"

Tiny pencil. Clipboard. "Quality of child supervision." *Check.*

"It was *for science,*" Sadie cried, but the woman didn't even care.

"Was it for science class?" she asked.

"Well, no, but —"

"I thought not. Since you obviously don't go to school."

Sadie actually gasped. "Of course I go to school!" April had never heard her sound so offended.

"Then why aren't you in school right now? At" — she looked at her watch — "ten forty-five on a weekday?"

It was a weekday? Honestly, April hadn't known. Days,

weeks, months . . . they only kept track of how many passed, not what they were. Lately, every day was a day that ended in *why hasn't Izzy come home?*

The woman raised an eyebrow, as if she had just won an argument with a twelve-year-old, and where could she pick up her trophy.

So that's why April said, "We were just on our way there. To school. To do . . . schooling. Right now."

"Really?" Ms. Pitts sounded doubtful. "And who exactly teaches this school?"

For an embarrassingly long time, no one answered. And then Colin stepped on Gabriel's foot. Hard.

"Ow!" Gabriel said, but a second later, he caught on and said, "I do."

"Excellent." The woman gripped her clipboard tighter. "Then don't let me keep you. Let's see this school. And while we're there, perhaps I can speak one-on-one with some of the children?" she asked, but every kid there was smart enough to know it wasn't really a question.

"Your name?"

"Colin."

"Colin what?" As soon as they got upstairs to

the schoolroom, the woman had slipped on a pair of glasses that looked to be at least fifty years old. They matched her old-fashioned watch and old-fashioned pencil and old-fashioned hair that still had bits of eggshell in it.

"Your last name, Colin?" the woman asked again.

"That depends who's asking," Colin said, but Ms. Pitts looked confused, so he added, "I've had a few."

"Elaborate," the woman ordered, because she obviously didn't understand Colin or the short con that had turned into a long con as soon as Colin's mother took off, abandoning Colin and leaving him at Winterborne House for good.

"You see, love, I used to live a life of crime. Different towns. Different names. You might even say that I've never known stability or safety until I came to Winterborne House."

It was his best con artist voice. April knew it when she heard it, but the woman didn't sound impressed.

"You arrived more than a year ago, is that correct?" she asked.

"A fact for which I thank the good Lord every day," he said, laying it on a little thicker.

"But Winterborne House isn't the same *now,* is it?" she asked pointedly. "Things are . . . shall we say . . . under new management?"

On the other side of the schoolroom, Gabriel was trying to pull down an old-fashioned map that hung suspended from the ceiling. But it wouldn't stay down. Every time he turned it loose, the map would roll quickly back up, springing just out of his grasp.

"Oh, *Mr.* Winterborne," the woman called across the room, "what is our lesson for the day?"

The map sprang up again, but this time Gabriel caught it. He grabbed a pair of scissors off the table then slammed the blades through the map and into the wall, and the map stayed down at last.

"Geography," Gabriel replied coolly.

"Excellent," the woman said.

But when he asked, "Is everyone ready?" April knew what he was really saying was, *Play along. Don't screw this up.*

The kids all filed in and sat at the table as if they did this every day, and, perhaps for the first time, Ms. Pitts might have looked impressed.

"We use a mode of immersive learning here at Winterborne House," Gabriel said to the woman's confused face.

"I see," she said in the manner of someone who didn't see at all. "Do go on, Mr. Winterborne. I'm interested to see your lesson in . . . geography, was it?"

"Yes."

"Well . . . uh . . . class, this is Gorod." He turned to the map and pointed to a small country near the Adriatic Sea. "It's about three hours from the Adrian border by car. Or nineteen by donkey. I don't recommend the donkey. Anyway . . . very remote. Very rural. Their money is called the Koin, but since the fall of the iron curtain, their real currency has been power." April could feel his confidence growing. "A few well-placed bribes in the right hands, and you can—"

Colin cleared his throat loudly and jerked his head in the social worker's direction.

Instantly, Gabriel remembered. "Explore the rich culture of this wonderful destination."

"Hmmm," the woman said, then picked up her tiny pencil.

"Ms. Pitts, did you have a question?" Gabriel asked her.

"Are you living here alone with the children, Mr. Winterborne?"

"Yes," Gabriel said simply.

The woman flipped over a piece of paper on her clipboard. "According to our records, there is supposed to be a servant in residence?"

Gabriel nodded. "Smithers is in on holiday. He'll be home soon."

"And your uncle?" the woman asked, but Gabriel huffed.

"As we established downstairs, my uncle lives in jail." Gabriel smiled.

"Was *he* in contact with the children?" Ms. Potts clarified, and hopefully didn't hear Colin mumble, *"Only when he was trying to kill us."*

But Gabriel was cool as could be. He actually smiled at the woman. "As you said, the home used to be under different management."

"Where is Isabella Nelson?"

It was worse than the egg. Than the pancake. Than every awkward, embarrassing, infuriating thing that had happened since Ms. Gladys Pitts set foot inside Winterborne House. And she just stood there with her clipboard and her tiny pencil, not caring at all that she'd just asked the one question they had no idea how to answer.

"Mr. —"

"Traveling," Gabriel snapped. "Izz—Ms. Nelson is traveling."

"Traveling where?"

"We just got a postcard from her. From Dublin," Sadie said helpfully.

"Is that so?" the woman said. "How lovely. And how unfortunate."

"Unfortunate how?" April had to ask.

The woman was still standing, wandering around the room that was dustier than Smithers would have ever allowed. She seemed almost bored as she said, "It took months for Ms. Nelson and the foundation to become a qualified foster care provider."

"I'm in charge of the foundation now," Gabriel countered.

"And the children?" She looked him up and down. "Are you in charge of them? Because I must say—"

"The children are fine right here," Tim told her.

"Are you?" the woman asked, then picked some egg-shell off her sweater. "I suppose we'll see." She started for the door. "Well, I'd hate for you all to miss any of this stimulating lecture, so I'll see myself out. But rest assured, you'll be hearing from me, Mr. Winterborne." She stopped and looked back. "I suggest you start opening your mail."

And then she was gone, out the door and down the hall, and soon the sound of her sensible heels clicking on the hardwood floors couldn't be heard at all.

"Tim?" Gabriel said.

"Follow her and make sure she actually leaves?" Tim guessed.

Gabriel nodded, and Tim took off like a shot, and for a second, it was like all the oxygen in the room went with him.

When Gabriel muttered, "Class dismissed," no one had the heart to say that it hadn't been a class at all. It was a test. And April sat there for a long time, terrified of the answers.

FOUR

THE INVITATION

April should have been hungry. But she wasn't. Before she'd come to Winterborne House, she'd been hungry all the time, but that night she looked at the six different kinds of soup that came from what Sadie called "Smithers's emergency cabinet," and none of it looked even a little bit appealing.

Maybe she was getting sick. Or maybe, on some level, she just knew enough to be worried. And it wasn't just because someone had tried to salvage the cake and it sat in front of them like a brick wall with icing as mortar.

"*Mmmmm.* Looks so *goooood,*" Violet tried, forcing a smile in Gabriel's direction.

"I'm sorry. It was supposed to look . . . different."

"It's fine," Tim said quickly.

"No. That's not how it looked in the picture."

"I'm sure it tastes fine," Tim said. (It didn't taste fine.)

"I'll get baking powder when I go to the store."

"Gabriel?" Sadie asked.

"Yeah?"

"It's okay if you don't want me to, but there's a grocery store that delivers, and I could set it up. All we'd need is a credit card number, and—"

"Oh, I know the credit card nu . . ." But Colin trailed off when Gabriel glared in his direction.

"Nothing. I know nothing," Colin said, then took another bite of tomato soup.

"Fine," Gabriel said after a moment.

"What?" Sadie asked.

"Do that. Whatever. Order whatever you want, Sadie. I don't care."

He really didn't; April could tell. That was even sadder. And scarier. Because she'd been in the system for ten long years, and if there was one thing April had learned, it was that indifference wasn't always a blessing.

But Sadie didn't know that. She'd gone from two parents who loved her to a grandmother who adored her to

Ms. Nelson and Smithers, who would have done anything to keep her safe.

She didn't see the danger in Gabriel's shrug and the mumbled words, "Spend whatever. Buy whatever. I don't care."

Sadie didn't know. But Tim did. And April met his eyes across the table.

"Do you mean clothes and things too?" Sadie went on, not believing her luck. "Because Violet still needs—"

"Yes. Just . . . Whatever you need. I don't care. Money, I have."

No one asked him what he *didn't* have, maybe because they were half afraid that he would answer, so everyone went back to their soup.

"That awful woman didn't know what she was talking about," April said. "This is the best place I've ever lived, Gabriel. Ever."

"Yeah," Tim agreed. "Me too."

"They're not gonna take us away," Sadie told him. "They couldn't. They wouldn't! You're . . . We're . . . They won't take us away! We'll keep an eye out for the next notice, and in the meantime, I'm going to make a chore wheel and we'll all take turns cleaning and organizing, and Smithers and Izzy left lesson plans, so we can start . . . They won't take us away!" she said one last time, but it sounded like the person she was trying to convince was herself.

"Of course not." Gabriel forced a smile. "Now, eat up," he said, and they all went back to their soup except for Colin, who was going through the mail, making stacks. "Credit card application. Might want to hang on to—"

"Colin," Gabriel growled.

"We can shred that," Colin said, sliding the paper into another pile, then going back to the big stack. "Bill. Bill. Ooh." Colin held a pink envelope up to his nose and took a sniff. "Perfume. Someone has an admirer."

But Gabriel just shrugged and said, "Shred it."

"Bill," Colin said, going on. "*Scientific Weekly.*" He slid the magazine over to Sadie. "Bill." And then he stopped. For a long moment, he didn't say anything at all. He just looked down at the thick envelope in his hands. Even from the other side of the table, April could tell that this wasn't junk mail. Definitely not a bill. The envelope looked rich and expensive, more like fabric than paper. But it was the return address that made everyone at the table go quiet.

The Winterborne Foundation.

"Well, what have we here?" Colin said before slicing open the envelope and pulling out a thick card. Suddenly, the words *gala* and *benefit* and *museum* were too bright for April. She didn't want to look at them because, if she did, she might be reminded that she'd been in the museum when it burned. And that it might have been a teeny-tiny bit her fault. (Just a little.)

So, obviously, April didn't want to linger too long over that particular piece of paper. But Gabriel was the opposite. He kept staring at the invitation, one finger running over the bottom like it held the secret to the universe.

"You know, it's just a piece of paper. It can't hurt . . ." But April trailed off when she saw the name on the invitation: Isabella Nelson.

Then Gabriel just got up.

And walked away.

April helped Tim and Violet clear the table. Then while Colin washed and Sadie dried, April put the dishes away, but, mostly, April just stood there, missing Smithers. And

Izzy. Because Smithers would have known what to say to Gabriel. And Izzy would have just slapped him upside the head and told him to get over whatever it was that was bothering him. Then he would have done exactly that.

"So, movie night?" Sadie asked with a gleam in her eye as soon as they put away the last of the dishes. "I put popcorn on the list, but we can still watch something. I'm feeling rather Pixar-y."

Everyone started for the door, but when they reached the home theater, April lingered in the hallway just outside.

Tim looked back at April. "You coming?"

"No. Maybe. I mean . . . I forgot something."

He didn't ask what. He just nodded and said, "Okay. Let us know when you find him."

But April didn't find Gabriel.

Not in the room Smithers called the sitting room (even though, in April's opinion, it had the most uncomfortable chairs).

He wasn't in the room where he slept or the room where he was supposed to sleep but had never moved into because it once belonged to his mom and dad.

Gabriel wasn't in the library. Or the laundry. Or the conservatory that didn't actually conserve anything, even though Smithers did his best to keep the plants green all throughout the heart of winter.

She searched the study (though what Gabriel studied she didn't really know) the music room (where absolutely no one ever played any music), and the butler's pantry (that was 100 percent butler-free).

She even searched the cellars where he'd hidden and lived and nearly died.

But Gabriel Winterborne was nowhere to be found.

She was going up the library stairs to search the balcony again when she heard a scraping sound below.

By then, April should have been used to the sight of the big stones in the library floor dropping down, spiraling into darkness, forming a staircase that led to the Winterborne family's greatest secret—and legacy. But it always felt a little bit like magic, and that night, for some reason, she stayed especially still and quiet, not wanting to break the spell as a figure in a black shirt and sleek leggings emerged from the secret chamber. She could just make out the features of Gabriel's face before he settled a cape (yes! a cape!) around his shoulders and pulled a big black hat low over his brow.

April's breath caught. Because he wasn't Gabriel

Winterborne anymore. He was the Sentinel. And he was heading for the doors.

April ran down the spiraling stairs and across the library just in time to see him stroll across the dimly lit back patio and start down the steps that zigzagged over the cliffs to the rocky shore below. She peered over the edge just as the lights of the boathouse flipped on. A moment later there was a roar as a boat floated out into the ocean and headed toward town.

At that point, April wasn't thinking anymore. She was turning. And running back into the house and down the halls and then throwing open the door to the home theater.

She jumped forward, into the projector's flickering light as she shouted, "It's happening! He's doing it. He's Sentineling!"

"I don't think that's really a verb," Colin said, but Tim bolted upright.

"When?" he asked.

"Now."

FIVE

SPRINGTIME

April had never really minded the dark. It wasn't that she could see in it. (She wasn't a cat.) It wasn't even so much that she was at home in it. (Hello, there are things in the dark. And a lot of them bite!) But darkness had always been a way of life for April. All the better for sneaking and swiping and taking care of whatever it was that needed to be done. But, more than anything, night was when the monsters came out, so wasn't that the best time to fight them?

Or so April told herself as she hunkered low and ran along the outcropping of rocks by the pier.

Tim had docked their boat not far from Gabriel's — so he was there. Somewhere. She and Tim and Colin couldn't have been more than ten minutes behind him. The motor of his boat was still warm, so he couldn't have gotten far.

But a heavy fog was rolling in off the water, and the moon was hidden behind a thick layer of clouds. A freezing wind blew off the ocean, cold and wet and smelling a lot like very salty snow. But April didn't dare slow down because she had a mission on her mind.

And a voice in her ear, saying, "Springtime, do you have eyes on the subject?"

April rolled her eyes, thankful that Tim and Colin had convinced Sadie that she and Violet should stay back at the house to monitor the comms units that no one but Sadie even wanted to use anyway. "I don't like that code name."

"Well, do you have a better idea? Over."

"I don't think we have to say *over*," Colin said. Then added, "Over."

"Springtime?" Sadie asked again.

"You could call me April," April said.

"No. Sadie's right," Colin said.

"Thank you, James Bond," Sadie said.

"I *really* don't like that code name," Tim muttered.

"Too bad," Colin said. "I'm suave. Debonair. And

licensed to ki—Oops." That's when Colin tripped over a rock. "I'm okay!" he shouted.

"You were saying, Super Spy?" Tim asked him.

But Sadie was in their ear, snapping, "Does anyone have eyes on the subject?" and April remembered they had work to do.

She could just imagine the look in Sadie's eyes as she watched the monitors and tracked the dots that represented the three of them. They didn't have a dot for Gabriel, though. And that was the problem.

"I knew I should have tagged all that vintage Sentinel stuff with a tracker," Sadie said for what must have been the dozenth time since April had come bursting in, interrupting movie night. "I thought I could get him to use my inventions, but *noooooo*. I bet that cape isn't even fire-resistant. I could whip something up in a week if he'd just let me."

Tim and April looked at each other. They did *not* want to think about the tests that would go into any fireproof inventions that Sadie might be dreaming up.

But they had bigger problems at the moment. Gabriel was out there. Somewhere. Doing . . . something. And he might get hurt. He might need help. Sure, members of the

Winterborne family had been dressing as the fabled Sentinel and fighting crime for generations. Gabriel himself had studied fencing since he was a kid, and he'd spent ten years on the run, fighting and surviving and training for vengeance. But this was his first time being an official superhero and, at the very least, April wanted to see him in action.

The dock was small with dingy bulbs hanging overhead, leading from the boats to a deserted parking lot on her right—and, beyond that, a larger street and the busier parts of the city. But it was what was on April's left that made her stop and pause. Darkness and cliffs, rocks and trees. April was 90 percent sure that it was some kind of park, but it felt more like a black hole—an abyss. And she wasn't sure which path was the scariest as she stood there, considering their options.

She was just getting ready to suggest that maybe she and Tim and Colin should split up to cover more ground when Violet's voice came through the SadieSonic devices that they all wore in their ears.

"Um . . . guys. I think someone might be . . . out there. On your left."

April froze and searched the shadows. There was the

cold wind and a low hum as the SadieSeer 600 hovered overhead, Violet at the controls. April felt Colin at her back.

But it was Tim who said, "I see him."

In the distance, the shadows moved, a black form sweeping like a piece of paper being blown by the wind between the rocks and trees.

April had watched him train. She'd seen him fight. She knew Gabriel Winterborne, but there was something otherworldly in the way he crept through the darkness. April must not have been the only one to sense it, because the three of them were super extra careful as they climbed up the steep ridge and over the uneven ground. More than once, April thought she might have turned back if she had been alone. Because there was something coming over her, stronger and colder than the wind. She just knew that the pier was disappearing behind her and a Sentinel-shaped shadow was moving through the night in front of her while the clouds stayed thick overhead, blocking out the light of the moon.

A stone fence stood in the distance, tall and menacing, and April wasn't surprised when, once they reached it, Gabriel was nowhere to be seen.

"You don't think he . . . climbed that, do you?" Colin asked, but Tim just laughed.

"Have you met Gabriel?" Tim asked.

"Fair point," Colin grumbled as April pushed him aside and ran her hands along the rocks, feeling for grooves.

"Someone give me a boost."

"Now, Springtime," Colin said, "let's not be too hasty." But Tim's hands were already under April's right foot, giving her just enough of a push that she could grip the rough, cold stones on the top of the wall.

"That's probably not a good idea," Colin warned.

But April was kicking and pulling. Her fingers were burning, and an unease was churning in her stomach like maybe she'd eaten something she really should have left alone.

"April," Colin whispered, "we don't know where we are."

But as she peeked over the top of the wall, April swallowed hard and had to admit, "Actually . . . I do."

The smoke was gone, but April could almost smell it, mixing with the salt from the sea, swirling in the foggy air as she looked at a building that she'd last seen engulfed in flames. The newspapers had said it was totally destroyed, but the papers, it seemed, were wrong because one wing remained. Soft golden light fell through tall windows, and everything looked shiny and fresh and new.

"April, are you gonna tell us what you see or aren't—"

"The museum, Sadie. We're at the museum."

"The one you burned down?" Colin asked as April finally pushed herself high enough to rest atop the wall.

"Yeah." April's eyes scanned the museum's grounds. "That's the one."

"What's Gabriel doing here?" Sadie asked, but Tim was already boosting Colin up onto the wall beside April and saying, "There's one way to find out."

SIX

THE SENTINEL'S RETURN

The closer April got to the museum, the harder her heart pounded, and it wasn't just because she was running. Fast. At night. On the heels of a billionaire-slash-aspiring-vigilante. Toward a building that she had semirecently set on fire. At least, it wasn't entirely that.

Because while part of the museum was shiny and clean with a fresh coat of paint, it wasn't hard to see where the other part used to be. It was like a piece of burned toast with the black parts scraped off, and April could have lived without the reminder. She didn't like thinking about the fire or the smoke or the way the whole world had gone topsy-turvy just before she'd passed out. She really didn't like to think about the Sentinel-shaped figure that had carried her to safety.

April had spent weeks assuming it was Gabriel, but he swore it wasn't him, so sometimes April wondered if maybe there really was a benevolent ghost out there somewhere, saving wayward little girls when they did something stupid. But April knew better than to count on it. Where April came from, girls almost always had to save themselves.

So she hunkered low and ran faster across the lawn. Light beamed through the windows, and something floated on the air. Something that sounded a lot like . . .

"Music?" Colin stopped and looked around. "Does anybody hear —"

"There!" Tim was pointing at the building, high up, at the place where a black cape billowed in the light breeze that floated off the sea and over the balcony that ran along the building's upper story.

"How'd he get up there?" Colin asked.

"He's Gabriel Winterborne," April said with a shrug.

And then she started to climb.

Or she meant to.

Really, she did.

If Gabriel could climb that high wearing a cape, of all things, surely April — the best climber in any home she'd ever been—could make it. She was even wearing her good shoes. But April was no more than a foot or two off the ground when arms grabbed her around the waist and pulled her from the building's wall.

"Hey!" she cried, trying to spin around and yell at Tim. But it's hard to spin when you can't touch the ground, she discovered. "Come on. If Gabriel can make it—"

"April—"

"Do you want to help Gabriel or don't you?"

Tim dropped her, then pointed toward Colin, who was holding open a door and sweeping out a hand, and saying, "After you."

It must have been some kind of emergency exit because the walls were white and the stairs were metal and the clanging of their footsteps echoed as they ran, up and up to the top floor before creeping into a long corridor on the same level as the balcony. The carpet was red and thick, and their feet didn't even make a whisper of a sound. But she still found herself wishing that the shadows would come back.

Glossy, shiny light fixtures hung overhead. Wall sconces glowed between windows surrounded by deep red draperies. Everything smelled like new paint, and April's head hurt, but at least nothing was on fire, and April was willing to take that as a win.

"Okay," April said softly. "Sadie, we're in. We're gonna split up and find Gabriel. But we're not going to engage. Right?"

"Hey, we're not the ones I'm worried about," Colin pointed out.

"Fine. *I* won't engage," April said. And she meant it. She didn't cross her fingers or anything. "We're just gonna find Gabriel and—"

"Uh . . . guys?" Tim was standing in the shadows at the edge of the room, peeking over the railing and looking down on the floor below. His voice sounded almost wary when he said, "Remember the invitation to that fancy party? I think it must have been a *costume* party."

"What makes you say . . ." But April trailed off as she saw Gabriel walking up the sweeping stairs. It took all of her willpower not to call out. Suddenly, Colin grabbed her by the arm and pulled her to the floor, then pushed her toward the shadows and the shelter of a potted plant that stood beside the railing.

"What are you—" she started, but Tim jerked his head, and she followed his gaze, through the balustrade and over the edge to the crowded floor below, and that's when she saw Gabriel over by the buffet . . . Or was that him talking to the woman by the door? There were Gabriels everywhere!

No. Not Gabriels, April realized. *Sentinels.*

It must have been the most popular costume in town, because every two feet there was another man in a long black cape and big black hat, with a sword and a mask.

April watched people dance and mingle while waiters circled with silver trays.

"Gabriel snuck out to come to a costume ball?" she said, feeling numb and foolish and more than a little confused. That really wasn't like the Gabriel she knew.

"A ball!" Sadie cried through the earpieces. "Ooh. Are there dresses?"

"Is there fancy food?" Violet asked.

"Is Gabriel dancing?" Sadie asked with glee.

"Every third man here is dressed like the Sentinel, Sade," Colin informed her. "So, yeah. A whole lot of Gabriels are dancing. But there's no way to know which one he really is."

"This doesn't make any sense," April couldn't help but say. "He wouldn't come to a ball. Why would he . . ."

And then April stopped.

And froze.

Because, down below, one of the Sentinels was calling, "Izzy!"

And then the man was taking off, pushing through the crowd like he didn't care how many waiters he cut off or how many hems he stepped on as he barreled his way across the floor and reached for a woman with sleek black hair and a long white dress.

"Izzy?" April heard herself ask.

"Izzy's there?" Sadie shouted, and April didn't quite know how to answer, because April didn't want to get her hopes up. That was the worst possible place for hopes to be! She'd learned that lesson a hundred times, but April was already leaning closer to the railing, desperate to hear every word.

"I thought she was traveling. I thought she was away. I thought she . . . left us," Sadie said.

"She did leave us," Tim said. "She's not here."

"You don't know that," Sadie said.

"Yeah. We do," Colin said.

"But how —"

"Because Gabriel is *not happy*." Colin pointed to where

the woman in the white dress was walking away from the man who had to be Gabriel.

In hindsight, he should have been easy to spot. The other Sentinels at the gala were playing dress-up, but this wasn't a game to Gabriel. It was a calling. A birthright. And he seemed more on guard at this party than he had on his uncle's rooftop, fighting for his life.

"He's not even eating the tiny shrimp," Colin said. "What kind of monster passes up tiny shrimp?"

Gabriel stood on the edges of the party, scanning the room like he might look at a field of battle. He was marking the exits and identifying the threats—which came in all shapes and sizes it turned out, because when a woman in a slinky dress walked up to him, April was half afraid he might draw his swords.

When the woman touched his arm, he flinched, then brushed her aside and pushed his way across the dance floor.

"She's not here."

April heard the words, but she didn't recognize the voice. She wasn't even sure who'd said them until Gabriel stopped and spun on a man who, it turned out, was standing right below where the kids were perched, straining to hear every word.

"Excuse me?" Gabriel said.

"You were looking for Isabella Nelson, weren't you? She's not here tonight, Mr. . . ." The man trailed off, waiting for Gabriel to say . . .

"I'm Gabriel Winterborne."

"Oh, wow! Cool! It's nice to meet you." He held out his hand. "Reggie Dupree. I've heard a lot about you."

"Is that so?" Gabriel asked.

"Yes. I'm a good friend of Izzy's."

"Oh boy," Tim and Colin said in unison as, down below, Gabriel was looking at the other man's hand as if deciding whether or not he should slice it off.

Eventually, he took it, but then the stranger winced, and Gabriel let go. "That's quite a grip you've got there. So how do you know Izzy?"

"Izzy and I . . . we . . . I mean to say—she's . . ."

"The love of his life?" Colin whispered, but down below, Gabriel struggled to say . . .

"An old friend." Sadness filled his eyes. "She's my oldest friend."

"Well, I'm going to do you a favor, Gabe, and not tell Izzy you called her old."

The stranger laughed. Gabriel scowled. And the other man laughed harder.

"Wow. You're really taking this costume seriously, huh?" The stranger brandished an invisible sword. "Stand and deliver!"

"I'm not a highwayman. I'm the Sentinel."

It was the first time April had ever heard him say the words aloud, but the moment was ruined by the grin on the other man's face as he slapped Gabriel on the back and said, "Oh, I know exactly who you are."

The moment stretched out a little too long and the silence between them was a little too loud and April was starting to worry, right up until the point when Gabriel said, "Where is Isabella?"

"Uh . . . not here. Didn't I say that? I thought I said that."

Gabriel took a step forward, slow and menacing despite the bright lights and tiny food on shiny platters. "Where is she?" he asked again, but this time it sounded more like an order.

Then, for the first time, Reggie Dupree stopped

smiling. "If she wanted you to know," he said slowly, "seems like maybe you would."

"Oooh. Please tell me he didn't wear his good swords," Colin said, and April leaned farther over the rail. She couldn't help it. She didn't want to miss a single word.

Then the stranger pulled a shrimp off a passing tray and plopped it in his mouth and said, "I'm afraid I've gotta scoot, but it's been swell talking to you, Gideon."

"It's Gabriel."

"Of course it is!" He gave Gabriel's arm a friendly pat. "So glad I got to meet you. Quite a night. And this *cos-tume!*" the man exclaimed. "Oh my gosh. I'd think you were the real Sentinel if I didn't know any better. Where'd you get it?"

"Oh, you know . . . Winterborne House is full of old treasures. Turns out my ancestors have been playing dress-up for centuries."

And then the stranger walked away.

"Come on. Let's go home." April felt Tim move back from the railing, farther into the shadows, but April didn't dare budge from that place. She wanted to keep an eye on Gabriel. He might need her. He might need them. Two things had kept him going for ten long years: wanting to stop Evert and needing to love Izzy, and now both of those things were lost to him—maybe forever—and he looked like April felt when she sat in the teacher's chair and Colin spun her around and around—like he had no idea how to make the world stop whirling.

"April?"

"Will he be okay?"

"Of course he will," Tim said "He's Gabriel. He's allowed to be out after dark. Unlike us, so we've got to—"

Down below, the band stopped playing. The lights went out. And a spotlight sliced through the darkness, onto a stage.

"Ladies and gentlemen!" A man in funky glasses and a hot pink tuxedo jacket had a microphone, and his voice boomed throughout the room. "Thank you so much for being here to help us raise money for the new—and much improved—museum."

"Let's go," Tim whispered, but before April could budge, she heard a noise coming from the shadows.

The ding of an elevator followed by a rattle. A whisper. There was feedback from a walkie-talkie, then a gravelly voice saying, "I'm on the third floor, checking that silent alarm. Looks like someone came through the emergency exit."

April's heart didn't know whether it should go into overdrive or stop beating altogether as she heard the staticky reply: "Okay. Just do a quick sweep. Probably one of the caterers, but we've got to check it out."

"Okay," the first guard said.

Down below, the man in the pink jacket was still talking. No one was more surprised than April when he said, "We have a very special guest with us tonight. I wonder if we can get him to say a few words. The Winterborne Foundation is our platinum sponsor, after all, so come on, folks, put your hands together for Gabriel Winterborne!"

And Gabriel . . . Gabriel stood there looking like he was contemplating setting the place on fire. Again.

"Don't be shy, Mr. Winterborne. Come on up."

Someone pushed Gabriel toward the spotlight and the stage, and he looked like he wanted to fight—to run— but eventually he was standing in the glare, microphone in his hand.

At first, the crowd was silent. Everyone knew about Gabriel Winterborne. As a boy, he'd been rich and famous, cherished and beloved. But then the boy ran away, and no one seemed to know what to think about the man who had come back.

There was a polite smattering of applause followed by an awkward silence before Gabriel managed to say, "Hello."

Overhead, the guard's footsteps were getting closer, so April pulled Tim behind some fancy fabric thing that hung from the ceiling and ran down a pillar and then draped all the way to the floor.

"Okay. Now we're trapped in here instead of out there," Tim said, but, outside, the footsteps were getting louder as the guard drifted closer.

April parted the fabric and peeked out at the man, who eyed the emergency exit and pulled the door solidly shut. They couldn't get out that way, but they had to get out! So April dropped the fabric and leaned back against the pillar and tried to think.

On the other side of the pillar, that level was dark and empty. There would be more doors. More stairs. If only she and Tim could just get to the other side . . . If only . . .

Then April had an idea. (Which was a good thing.) But it was a very April-ish idea. (Which was frequently a bad thing.) But she didn't let that stop her.

"What are you doing?" Tim snapped when April threw a leg over the railing.

"We can get out the other side. We just have to get around the pillar."

"April!"

"No one will see," she said. "It's dark. We just have to climb over, slip around the pillar, and we can leave from the other side. Come on."

"April!" Tim grasped her sleeve, but she was already on the outside of the railing. She just had to reach . . . She just had to stretch . . . She just had to slip around the pillar and back onto the balcony . . .

But, by that point, April was just slipping.

"Thank you for coming. I'm . . . uh . . . Gabriel. Gabriel Winterborne . . ."

Down below, Gabriel was fumbling for words, but overhead, April was fumbling for a grasp. Her shoe must have gotten tangled in the pretty, drapey fabric, and when she tried to place a foot between the balustrades of the railing, it slipped and April winced. She grabbed on to the frilly fabric like it was a lifeline, and for a moment, she dangled there.

"April!" Tim stretched over the railing, but April was too far to reach.

Cries went up from the crowd, gasping and murmuring as the fabric pulled away from where it was pinned to the pillar and April went swinging across the ballroom like the worst Tarzan ever, knocking over flower arrangements and an ice sculpture that stood on a pedestal in the center of the room. And then she was swinging back in the other direction.

"Catch her!" someone yelled, but the fabric ripped, and April wasn't swinging anymore. She was falling.

The crowd parted. People screamed. And April braced for impact, but the impact didn't come, as she found herself in a pair of strong arms. (Which was a good thing.) But then she looked up into Gabriel's glaring eyes. (Which was a bad thing.)

Gasps and cries filled the air, but Gabriel didn't move as he stood glaring down at April, whose body wasn't nearly as bruised as her pride.

"And this is April," Gabriel told the crowd, as if that should have been explanation enough.

SEVEN

THE SECOND SENTINEL

April was sure that the distance between the museum and the dock hadn't doubled since the three of them had left on their little adventure. But it felt like it.

"*You*"—Gabriel pointed at April—"ride with me. Tim, you and Colin take the other boat, but stay close and try not to do anything stupid."

Now Gabriel stood behind the controls. Hat gone. Mask off. He'd balled the cape up and shoved it in some compartment, so he was almost the Gabriel she knew as he steered the boat across the water that was as dark and shiny as ink.

"Did I mention I'm sorry?"

"Not now, April," he said.

And then, for the first time, April realized something about him was just . . . wrong.

The clouds parted, and for one split second, moonlight shone upon him and she knew.

"Are those swords . . . plastic?" No wonder he was acting surly. Generations of Winterbornes were probably rolling over in their graves. "You went out with *plastic swords!*"

But Gabriel didn't even look at her. "One does not wear Spanish steel to a party, April."

"Oh. Okay. Well, even without them, your costume was the—"

"It's not a costume," he snapped.

"I know!" April exclaimed. "That's why we thought . . ." She trailed off, half afraid to go on, when Gabriel spun on her.

"You thought what?" he asked slowly.

"We thought you might need us. You know. We were backup."

He shook his head and turned his gaze back to the water. "You're a thorn in my side is what you are. What were you thinking?"

"I was thinking about this!" April threw out her arms and gestured at the water that stretched all the way to the horizon. "Watching someone almost die is scary, you know. Pushing on their chest so you can keep their blood in their body? That's the kind of thing that stays with a girl." He started to argue, but April didn't give him the chance. "And don't worry. I know that was my fault too. Everything is my fault."

She dropped into her seat.

"I'm not your responsibility, April. You're mine." Then he leaned so close she might have thought he was going to hug her. Except . . . well . . . he wasn't exactly the hugging type. So she shouldn't have been surprised when he spoke right into the SadieSonic that had gone conspicuously quiet in her ear. "YOU'RE ALL MY RESPONSIBILITY!"

He turned back to the controls, and when he spoke again, it was like he was talking to the night. "Not that I asked for it."

That hurt more than the fall. More than the bruise on her leg from where she'd collided with the ice sculpture. More even than her pride. So she stayed quiet until the lights of the Winterborne family boathouse came into view.

"I'm hiring a blasted nanny," Gabriel mumbled to himself. "Or a zookeeper."

Then he maneuvered the boat into its slot and watched as Tim and Colin did the same. They tied them off, and Gabriel pointed to the stairs and the cliffs. "Now, go. Inside. All of you. Before it starts to rain."

But April didn't move. She couldn't, so she just said, "I really am sorry."

"Not as sorry as I am."

He didn't face her—couldn't look at her. It was like he was talking to the cold air, mumbling to the shadows. Like they weren't even there. Like he wished they weren't there at all.

"We—"

Colin grabbed her hand and finished for her: "Are going inside to think about what we've done!"

Tim's hand was steady on the flashlight as they started up the creaky stairs and rocky cliffs. The wind had turned colder, wetter. In the distance, the clouds were full of lightning, but April wasn't even a little bit afraid. Even when she stopped and glanced back down to the boathouse and the water.

"I was just trying to help."

"We know," Colin said.

"If he'd just let us—"

"We're not what he needs," Tim said.

They climbed on in silence for a moment. "She'll be back soon, right?" April didn't have to say who "she" was. Everybody knew.

"I couldn't tell ya," Colin told her. "Usually, I'm pretty good at reading people because, hello, family business. But I gotta say . . . I never could read her."

April understood what he meant. Ms. Nelson was kind. She was good. But April didn't really know her. She wondered if anyone did. And as much as April was certain that Isabella Nelson was going to come back someday, she had to remind herself that she'd spent ten years thinking her mom would come back, too. So April was very, very used to being wrong.

"That's weird," Tim said, and April banged into his back when he stopped.

"Pretty much everything in our lives is weird, Tim. You're gonna have to be more specific," she told him.

He pointed to the mansion where it stood at the top of the cliffs. "The lights are out."

Colin huffed and walked on. "Sadie's no fool. She and Vi probably went to bed before April even hit the floor.

No way they wanna incur the wrath of Gabriel if they can help it."

Colin crossed the back patio and pushed open the door, but April felt Tim tense. He wasn't wrong. The house was too dark. Too still.

As they eased inside, April tried to be quiet. She wanted to be careful. But then she stubbed her toe and almost fell—and she would have if Tim hadn't caught her.

Colin laughed, saying "Careful, love. Here. Let me get the . . ."

But when Colin flicked the switch on the wall, the lights stayed off and Tim started saying, "Violet. Where's Violet?"

There was another bang as April collided with something else.

"Ouch!" Colin exclaimed because, it turned out, that something was him.

"Where are Sadie and Violet?" Tim was starting to panic. April could hear it in his voice.

"I told you, they're probably in bed." Colin threw open a cabinet and grabbed two more flashlights, then handed one to April. "I'll go check the generator. Smithers used to have to wiggle the doohickey almost every time it stormed."

"It's not storming yet," Tim said, then bolted across the room. She heard him running down the hall, shouting, "Violet! Sadie!"

April started after him, but stubbed her toe again.

"Ouch! What in the . . ."

April swung her flashlight around and saw a chair lying on its side. In the distance, Tim was yelling, "Violet!" and April took off at a run.

But with every step, she grew more worried. Furniture was askew. Paintings were crooked on the walls.

And Tim's voice was getting frantic. "Sadie! Violet! Where are you? Violet!"

"Tim!" April yelled. "Where are you?"

"Library!" he shouted back, and April hurried for the doors.

Outside, the lightning was closer. Brighter. Bursts flashed through the glass windows and French doors, but in the library, all April saw was chaos.

Books everywhere. Chairs overturned. Tim was standing overhead, looking down from the balcony, frozen.

"What's going on?" April called up to him. "Where are they? Sadie! Vi—"

Then there was movement in the dark. April almost screamed until she recognized the big hat.

"Gabriel." She took a deep breath, and her heart started beating again. "I think we've been robbed," she said, but she heard nothing but a low, rumbling laugh.

And then April knew.

"You're not Gabriel," April said as the Fake Sentinel reached for a sword.

Her flashlight's beam glistened off the blade, and April could only yell, "Tim, no!" because he was already launching himself over the railing of the stairs and onto the Sentinel below. They both crashed to the floor, but the Sentinel was smooth and strong and, in a flash, rolled and sprung upright.

And reached for a *second* sword.

Lightning struck.

The patio doors blew open—too hard to have just been the wind, and a new light filled the doorway as Gabriel held up a lantern from the boathouse, sending a flickering yellow glow around the room.

"Gabriel!" April shouted as the Sentinel charged in his direction, swords drawn.

It was almost like watching Gabriel fight . . . *himself?*

He drew his sword and tried to parry the first blow, but the Sentinel's blade whipped through Gabriel's like it was . . . a toy.

"Plastic swords," April whispered to herself.

She heard him growl as the Sentinel laughed. Gabriel Winterborne had brought a prop to a sword fight, and all April could do was shout, "Gabriel!" and toss him one of the pokers from the fireplace.

He caught it with one hand, still holding the lantern with the other.

The Sentinel lunged and Gabriel deflected the blow with the poker, dancing, parrying. It looked like he was fighting his own shadow. Then, slowly, he set the lantern on the ground and drew a very real knife.

When the Sentinel charged again, Gabriel caught one of the swords with the poker and twisted, sending it flying. Then the Sentinel lunged and rolled over a table, but Gabriel sidestepped and blocked the door.

The Fake Sentinel was trapped but seemed as calm as

could be as he looked around and picked up . . . a book? And threw it at Gabriel, who quickly ducked, then had to laugh. "Missed," he said.

"Meant to," the Sentinel whispered.

And a moment later, April realized why. The book had banged against the wall, then ricocheted off and landed on an antique vase, which toppled over and landed on the abandoned lantern.

It was like watching the worst SadieMatic ever as the lantern tipped, sending flames across the rich carpet and up the thick velvet curtains with a *whoosh* that felt entirely too familiar.

"Not again!" April cried.

But it was too late. Fire was already dancing from one curtain to the next. Black smoke billowed, filling the room, as the Sentinel jumped and crashed through the patio doors.

Gabriel tore at the flaming curtains and dragged them out onto the wet flagstones and into the falling rain, but he didn't wait for the flames to die out before he started to run. To chase. To follow a sword-wielding intruder out into the storm.

"Gabriel!" April shouted after him, and for a moment,

she didn't actually think he'd stop. "Gabriel, we can't find Sadie and Violet!"

Behind her, Tim was shouting again. "Violet! Vi—"

But this time, in the stillness, someone answered. "We're in here!"

The voice was faint and muted, but it was also definitely Sadie's.

She saw the fact register on Gabriel's face and then he pushed past her, back into the ransacked room and toward the muted yells and soft thuds that echoed around a house that suddenly seemed too quiet.

"Help!" the soft cry came. "We're in here!"

"In where?" Tim shouted, spinning and looking, and that's when April saw it: a bookcase leaning against a wall.

No. Leaning against *a door*.

"Stand back," Gabriel snapped, then tossed the heavy bookcase aside as if it weighed nothing at all, and Violet and Sadie tumbled out of the small closet that April had never noticed before.

The lights flickered on just as Colin appeared in the doorway, asking, "What's going on?"

And April had to admit she really didn't know the answer.

EIGHT

THE DAGGER

The fire still burned in the fireplace, but the heat wasn't enough to fight the chilly wind that blew through the broken doors.

"Oh my gosh!" Sadie cried when she got her first look at the chaos. "April, what did you do?"

"I didn't do anything! The Sentinel did it," April said, and Sadie spun on Gabriel. "Not him. Another one."

"Tell me everything," Gabriel ordered, but Sadie and Violet shared a look as if they were just as confused as everyone else.

"Well, we were tracking you guys. And then the electricity went out, and I remembered that Smithers keeps a bunch of candles in that closet, so we came to get some, and—"

"First there was a noise," Violet added. "Remember?"

"Yeah," Sadie said. "That's right. I thought the storm might have busted another window, but when we got down here, the door slammed closed behind us. At first I thought it must have been a draft, but then it wouldn't open."

Tim hunkered down to get a good look at Violet. "Are you hurt?" he asked slowly.

Violet glanced back up at Sadie, then shook her head. "We're fine," Sadie said.

But Gabriel winced.

"Are you okay?" April asked.

"It's only a scratch," Gabriel said as he clutched his side. His black shirt was wet from the rain, or so April thought. But as usual April was wrong because rainwater wasn't red.

"You're bleeding," she said.

"It's a scratch," he snapped again.

"That's a lot of blood for just a scratch. Here. Let me."

He pointed the fireplace poker at her.

"You've done enough."

"Gabriel, we need to call an ambulance. And the police!" Sadie started for the phone on the other side of the room, but Gabriel blocked her way.

"No. It's not deep, and it didn't hit anything vital. Trust me."

"Gabriel, I understood not asking for help when people thought you were dead, but that could get infected," April said, pointing at his side.

"If you think I don't know how to sew myself up, you haven't been paying attention."

"Yeah. We know. But we've seen the literal scars, so we're also pretty sure you're not very good at it," April told him. Gabriel, being Gabriel, didn't care.

"I know one thing," Sadie said. "We need a distress signal. A big one. A . . ."

"She's gonna call it the SadieSignal," Colin whispered, just as Sadie cried . . .

"SadieSignal!"

"Toldya."

"I'm thinking three short blasts followed by one long blast," Sadie went on. There was a basket full of old toys and games by the door, and Sadie dug around in it, then pulled out a whistle and put it over Gabriel's neck. "Here."

"That's a whistle," he said.

"It's a prototype!" she said. "Three short. One long.

Anybody hears that, call the police!" Sadie declared. But Gabriel just growled.

He growled louder when Colin picked up the short sword that Gabriel had knocked from the Sentinel's hand and whipped it through the air, saying, "At least there's an upside. New sword!"

"That's a dagger," Gabriel snapped. "Do you not know the difference?" he asked, as if *that* was where he was failing as a guardian.

But when Colin tried to flip the dagger, Gabriel grabbed it out of the air. "What did I tell you about . . ." Gabriel started, but trailed off as he looked down at the hilt and the blade. He weighed it in his hand, like it belonged there, but when he tossed the dagger lightly from one hand to the next, the motion made him wince.

"At least let us take a look at that," April said. "If you don't want to tell the police—"

"We don't tell anybody. Anything."

"But—"

"For once in your life, April, leave it alone!"

A drop of blood landed on the floor. April saw it. But she didn't say another word. No one dared to. And when

Gabriel told them, "Go to bed. All of you. Now. The mess will still be here in the morning," April didn't even bother to argue.

"How you doing, Vi?" April asked thirty minutes later.

The storm was dying down, but April could still feel a charge in the air as she moved around their suite, getting ready for bed.

"I'm fine," Violet said, nestling down into the covers.

"Sadie?" April asked, but Sadie had other things on her mind.

"April, what happened?"

"We told you," April said. "The electricity was out. We thought it was the storm, so Colin went to look at the generator, but then the house was a mess, so Tim and I started looking for the two of you."

"No. Not here. At the gala," Sadie clarified.

"Oh." April felt guilty. "I made everything worse. *Again*. I mean, one minute he was talking to some guy about Ms. Nelson—"

"So Izzy *was* there?" Sadie didn't even try to keep her voice down.

"No," April said sadly. "But Gabriel obviously thought she would be. Wait. I thought you knew all this?"

"The electricity went out about that time," Sadie explained, scooting closer.

"Oh. Well, Izzy wasn't there, but Gabriel met this guy who was a friend of Izzy's. They talked for a while, and it was awkward. I mean, really awkward."

"What friend of Izzy's?" Sadie asked, sounding doubtful.

"His name was Reggie Dupree. He was handsome. Seemed nice enough. But . . . let's just say it's a good thing Gabriel had plastic swords, because there was a whole lot of testosterone floating around. Gabriel did that thing where he squeezed the guy's hand too hard and then the guy did the thing where he pretended he didn't remember Gabriel's name. Like I said . . . *testosterone*. Anyway . . . then the guy left, and they made Gabriel give a speech."

"Wait." Violet shot upright. "Gabriel gave a speech? Gabriel? Our Gabriel?"

"Yeah."

"Why?" Violet asked.

April shrugged. "He's the Winterborne."

"You think he needs help with his stitches?" Sadie asked.

"You think he'd come to us if he did?" April asked back, which must have been answer enough, because nobody said a word. And then April fell asleep and dreamed of daggers and lightning, fire and blood.

———

NINE

THE CALM AFTER THE STORM

There's a reason they say "calm before the storm" because, in April's experience, after the storm, things are hardly ever calm. At all.

The house that had looked messy the night before was a downright disaster in the light of day. Books were all over the library, whole shelves pushed over like a herd of wild animals had stormed across the second floor. Tables were overturned. Chairs were broken. Curtains were ripped and charred and wet with rain. Stray bits of broken glass still littered the library floor, and a cold wind blew through a half dozen broken windowpanes.

Part of April missed Smithers terribly. Another part was glad he wasn't there to see it, she thought as she stood with Violet and Sadie on the library balcony, looking down at the floor below.

"What—" April started.

"A—" Sadie added.

"Mess," Violet finished just as Tim and Colin appeared at the library doors.

"Violet," Tim called up to her, "don't you dare come down here."

"But—"

"There's glass everywhere. Go find some breakfast."

"I'm not hungry," she called back.

"Ow!" Colin cried, and shook a hand that was dripping with blood. A big piece of broken glass lay by his feet.

"I rest my case," Tim said.

"Fine!" Violet shouted, then stormed off in a huff.

Colin shook his head. "They grow up so fast."

"Where do we even start?" April asked as she and Sadie went down the spiral stairs.

Colin handed them each a dustpan. "Remember when Izzy was trying to find us a new house? Maybe we should just move there. That might be less work."

"Let's just get this over with," Tim snapped. He might have even growled, which wasn't like Tim at all.

"So . . ." April started slowly, "Tim . . . *how'd you sleep?*" She finished in a singsong tune as she started sweeping glass from beneath the shattered windows.

"Sadie, do we have anymore plywood?" Tim called over April's head, so she talked on.

"Because, you know, sleep is very important. I need a good eight hours, or I'm just a bear, and I can't help but notice—"

"What?" he snapped.

"What's wrong?"

"Look at this place!" Tim threw out his arms.

"I know," April said calmly. "It looks bad now, but we'll clean it up. It'll—"

"I'm not mad about the mess!"

"Then what are you mad about?"

"I'm not mad," he snapped. Then he seemed to realize how it sounded. "Last night someone locked Sadie and Violet in a closet and then they did this." He gestured to the ransacked room. "We don't know what they were looking for. We don't know if they found it . . . if they'll be back." The way he said it, April knew that last one was the problem. "Heck, we don't even know if Gabriel bled to death on the kitchen floor last night."

"Gabriel's not dead in the kitchen," a small voice said, and April turned to see Violet standing in the doorway with a piece of toast in one hand and jelly all over the other.

"See?" Colin said. "One question answered."

"Gabriel's not even here," Violet finished.

"What makes you say that, Vi?" April asked, and Violet licked her fingers.

"Had to make my own breakfast."

"He's probably still in bed." April thought about the knife wound and looked down at the drops of blood on the floor. Then she cut her eyes at Sadie, who seemed more subdued than usual. "Should someone go check on him?"

But no one volunteered, so April tried again. "Should someone who *didn't fall off a balcony and make a scene in front of half the city last night* go check on him?" Still no one answered, so April said, "Or, hey? Maybe *I* should do it since he's already mad at me?"

"Good point," Colin said. "Excellent notion. We'll be here when you get back. And don't worry, if we hear screaming, we'll ignore it."

"Thanks, Colin."

"Anytime, love. Now off you go, then."

So that was how April found herself climbing the stairs

and making her way to the room where Gabriel slept, a.k.a. the room next door to Izzy's. She was quiet on the stairs and silent in the hall, and when she reached the door, she stood outside for a long time, listening carefully, before she finally found the courage to knock, because waking Gabriel was a lot like waking a bear. You didn't want to do it, but if you had to, you needed to be out of clawing distance first.

"Gabriel?" she said softly, but no sound came from the other side. She knocked again, harder this time, and the door swung open on a groan of creaky hinges.

The bed was rumpled, with twisted sheets and a quilt on the floor, but it probably hadn't been made since Smithers left, so that didn't mean anything, April reminded herself as she crept toward the bathroom. The door was open, and there wasn't any steam on the mirror. No wet towels or dirty washcloths. And, most of all, no Gabriel. So April kept looking.

He wasn't in the conservatory or the music room or the garage. She didn't find him on the patio or in the home theater or the little bathroom that smelled like lemons and had a light with a burned-out bulb.

Winterborne House was massive, and April told herself

that she couldn't possibly have checked it all, but as she stood in the morning light, she couldn't shake the feeling that she had missed something very, very important. She just didn't, for the life of her, know what it could possibly be.

"April? April!"

It took her way too long to realize Colin was trying to get her attention. Which was a surprise, considering he was currently dragging the remnants of three broken chairs across the foyer floor.

"Scale of one to ten, how mad do you think Gabriel would be if we just piled all this up on the patio and set it on fire? Because I saw a bag labeled 'Smithers's Emergency Marshmallows,' and I'm thinking—"

"I can't find him," April blurted.

"What?"

"I can't find him. I can't find Gabriel."

April's hands were starting to tingle, and her heart was starting to pound, but Colin just looked at her and laughed.

"It's a big house, love. Don't worry. Eventually, he'll find us."

But then a scream broke through the air.

In a flash, Colin dropped the debris and they both ran

down the hall and through the kitchen and to the big room where Smithers kept all the supplies.

Tim was already there, his hands on Violet's shoulders, as he knelt in the doorway, looking up at her, saying, "What's wrong, Vi? What happened?"

"I'm fine. It's not mine. It just scared me."

"What's not yours?" Tim asked, and Violet turned and pointed behind her.

"The blood."

There was a big metal table in the center of the room. April had seen it dozens of times. That was where Smithers folded laundry or polished candlesticks. But right then it was covered with rags and paper towels, packages and bottles.

All of it stained a dark, deep red.

"April." Tim spoke slowly. "Did you find Gabriel?"

April barely heard him over the roaring in her ears, and she couldn't do anything except shake her head and stare at a little box labeled **SMITHERS'S EMERGENCY SEWING KIT** and a pair of bloody scissors.

"It doesn't mean anything," Colin said. "We already knew he was hurt. He was gonna have to sew up that scratch—"

"Does that blood look like it came from a scratch to you?" Violet snapped.

"Colin's right," Tim said.

"I am?" Colin asked.

"This doesn't change anything. We're gonna split up and look around and find him." He picked up a clear glass bottle with a big red handprint on the side. "He's crashed out somewhere. He's fine."

And then the doorbell rang.

For a second, they all just stood there.

"So . . . maybe he lost his keys?" Colin tried. But no one answered.

Instead, they ran out of the room and through the kitchen and down the hall. When they reached the foyer, however, Sadie was already throwing open the door.

And Gladys Pitts was saying, "Where is Gabriel Winterborne?"

TEN

They didn't invite her in, but that didn't stop the woman, who pushed inside, a sort of wild look in her eyes.

"Answer me," she snapped at Sadie. "Where is your guardian?"

Sadie looked at April, who blurted, "Busy." Because *we're not sure, but I assume he's somewhere sleeping off the stab wound he got from last night's armed intruder* probably wasn't going to win them any favors.

Then the woman seemed to register the disaster area that was post-invasion Winterborne House. Sure, the worst of the damage was confined to the library, but even in the foyer there were bits of broken glass. And a broken vase.

A picture that hung crooked on the wall. April wondered again what the Sentinel had been looking for.

"It's so good to see you again, Ms. Pitts." Colin gave his most charming smile. "But I'm afraid you've caught us at a bit of a bad time."

"I can see that," the woman said, pulling a newspaper from her giant handbag and pointing at a headline that spread across the entire page: WINTERBORNE WARDS "CRASH" MUSEUM GALA.

Which, as headlines go, wasn't terrible. But then April saw the picture: her lying in Gabriel's arms while dozens of the most influential people in the city gasped and glared in horror.

"Well, love, at least he caught her," Colin said, but Ms. Pitts didn't look even a little bit impressed.

"It wasn't Gabriel's fault," April said, but the woman was already wandering off, following the trail of debris.

April darted out in front of her, momentarily relieved that Colin hadn't had time to start the bonfire. Tim tried to block the doors. Even Violet threw her tiny body in the woman's path, but nothing could keep her from the library.

"Oh my!" the woman said when she reached it. "What on earth . . ." Then she looked down at the bloody bottle that Tim still held in his hand. "Explain," the woman commanded.

"Gabriel didn't do this," Sadie said.

"Yeah," April agreed. "He wasn't even here when it . . ." She trailed off before she could finish, but the damage had already been done. The woman was already reaching for her tiny pencil and scribbling on her clipboard, saying, "Leaves children unsupervised . . ."

"Hey!" Sadie sounded offended. "I'm a teenager!" (She wasn't.) "And I took a babysitting class at the Y and got a perfect score on the test." (She probably did.) "I have a certificate and everything," Sadie grumbled, but April didn't think the Department of Social Services—or maybe just Gladys Pitts—could have cared less about certificates.

She was too busy looking around at the chaos left over from the night before.

When she spied a broken vase, Colin pushed aside the largest shards and said, "We're redecorating."

"I see." The woman turned slowly. "I'll ask one more time: *where is Gabriel Winterborne?*"

In hindsight, it might not have been the end of the world. Things probably would have been just fine if Sadie hadn't turned to April and said, "Well? Where is he?" and if April hadn't seen the key in the fireplace, still inside the lock that opened the secret stairs to the secret lair that was home to the Winterbornes' incredibly secret legacy.

"April?" Sadie asked again. "Where's Gabriel?"

A little voice in April's head answered, *He's down there.* Obviously he was! She felt silly that she hadn't checked there first, but now it was too late, and she couldn't exactly explain that Gabriel was down in his secret room, probably sharpening his swords.

So, instead, she said, "Now's *not a good time*," and hoped Sadie could read between the lines. "I think he might be . . . occupied."

April couldn't help herself. She looked at the fireplace and the little key and the stones that would drop away, revealing the secret chamber and far more questions than any of them wanted to answer.

"Occupied how?" Ms. Pitts looked at April over the top of her glasses.

"That's what Colin told me!" April blurted, and when the woman turned to study Colin, April waved at him and pointed at the stones and the key. Instantly, his eyes went wide, and he said, "Oh . . . yeah . . . Gabriel likes to go swimming. In the ocean."

"It's forty degrees," the woman countered.

"Or running. That's it. I think he's running."

"Are you telling me that Gabriel Winterborne has left five children here. Alone. With no adult supervision. *Again?*"

Which was entirely too much for Sadie, who cried out, "I. Have. A. Certificate!"

"As impressive as that may be, Miss Simmons, it is hardly a substitute for proper supervision."

"I'm sure Gabriel will be back soon. You're welcome to wait. Hey," Colin said brightly, "it's time for our violin practice. You wanna watch? We only made glass break that one time, so I think we're getting pretty—"

"Just tell Mr. Winterborne his case is still on my desk. And I don't anticipate it will be going away anytime soon." They followed her to the door, where she stopped momentarily and slapped the newspaper into April's hands. "He's welcome to keep this. I have multiple copies."

And then she was gone, walking into the cool morning air and the bright sun.

Sadie slammed the door and turned the lock and said, "Now, what aren't you guys telling me?"

But April didn't answer. She just said, "Come on."

When April turned the key and watched the stones around the library fireplace fall away, her heart rate should have returned to normal. She should have felt relief as she walked down the dim steps into the secret lair and called out, "Gabriel! Have we got something to tell—"

But April couldn't finish. She couldn't even move because, if the upstairs rooms were cluttered and dirty, then the lair looked like a bomb had gone off.

Cabinets were thrown open.

Drawers had been dumped.

Dummies and swords and books were scattered all over the room.

And, worst of all, Gabriel was nowhere to be seen.

"I thought Gabriel was down here," Sadie said, looking around and sounding confused. "Where is he?"

"He isn't here, Sade," Colin said, then turned to look at April. "He isn't anywhere."

For a moment, the words lingered in the space that still smelled like dust and damp and history. Only Sadie seemed immune to the weight of them.

"Well, that's just silly." She rolled her eyes. "He has to be *somewhere!*"

ELEVEN

SCHRÖDINGER'S BILLIONAIRE

Gabriel Winterborne wasn't anywhere.

Not that they could find, even though they searched the entire mansion. Twice. They searched until morning turned into noon and noon turned into evening.

They called his name until their throats hurt. They walked down halls and up stairs until April had to go put on more comfortable shoes. They searched and searched and searched some more, but never found him.

Not in the cellar where he'd hidden for weeks. Not in the home theater, even though it had the most comfortable chairs in the house and a box labeled **SMITHERS'S EMERGENCY RAISINETS**.

Every little noise made April start. Anytime the old house creaked, April would dart up the stairs, hoping she might find him wandering around some abandoned room she'd never seen before. She walked through every secret passageway she knew about and looked for even more, but with every step and every shout and every passing second, only one thing became certain.

"He's not here. He's gone."

She dropped heavily onto one of the kitchen chairs and looked at Colin, who stood at the stove, stirring a pot of soup, wearing an apron that said **THE BUTLER DID IT. (HE DOES EVERYTHING.)**

But it was Sadie who said, "We don't know that. Not really."

"Yeah, Sade. We kind of do," Colin said.

"It's impossible to prove a negative. So we can never prove that he's not here. We can only prove if he *is* here."

"Which he isn't," Colin said.

"Exactly," Sadie proclaimed. "Now you get it."

"No." Colin shook his head. "I really don't."

"It's basic science," Sadie said. "He's both here and not here. Like that Austrian physicist who said you could put a cat in a box and if it's dead, it might still be alive, and if it's alive, it might be dead, but until you know—it's *both*."

Sadie was talking faster and faster, and when she

stopped, everyone looked at her like she . . . well . . . had a dead cat in a box.

"It's Schrödinger's cat!" she said as if everything suddenly made sense. "But with a billionaire. He's Schrödinger's billionaire."

"I am so glad we don't have any pets," Colin said, then took the soup off the stove.

April was in the process of setting the table when the back door slammed open, pushed by a cold wind that swept through the kitchen and made April's hair fly around her face.

Tim tossed a pair of gloves on the table and ran a hand over his too-long hair, little shards of white falling to the floor. For a moment, April thought it was even more broken glass, but then she heard it — the *ping, ping, ping* of sleet against a window. She could actually feel the cold that still clung to Tim and his thick coat.

"Is that snow?" Violet asked, crawling up on one of the chairs and swiping at Tim's icy shoulders.

"No, Vi. It's sleet."

"You're cold." She shivered, and he pulled her close.

"So?" Sadie asked, like she didn't dare to sound hopeful. "What did you find?"

Tim took off his coat and hung it on the back of a chair. "Do you want the good news or the bad news?"

"There's good news?" April asked, honestly surprised.

"I checked the boathouse. One of them's missing."

They all thought about that for a moment, before Colin asked, "Is that the bad news or the good news?"

But Sadie was already giving a big, huge sigh of relief. "That's great!"

"It is?" Colin asked.

"Of course it is. That means Gabriel's just running an errand or something. He'll be back by bedtime."

He wasn't back by bedtime.

The sun was down, and the sky was black. They'd boarded up the broken windows and locked all the doors, and April sat with Sadie and Violet, huddled around the fireplace in the little sitting room — the one that opened to the secret passageway and the cellar and the sea, but tonight the fireplace was full of dancing orange flames and the door was closed, making it the warmest room in the house.

"Look out! Look out! Coming through!" Colin yelled. A moment later, the door slammed open and a twin-sized mattress crashed through the doorway, landing on the floor in a dusty *plop*.

"What's that for?" Violet asked.

"We're sleeping in here tonight," Colin explained.

"We—like, all of us? Why can't we sleep in our own rooms?" April asked.

"Because, one, there's a sword-wielding madman out there. And there's our mysterious intruder, too!" Colin waited for a laugh that didn't come. "Just a little Gabriel Winterborne-y humor to lighten the mood."

"What's two?" April asked.

"The floor upstairs is too hard. Scooch over." Colin pushed the mattress forward, and Tim appeared behind him, dropping another mattress onto the floor.

"And the floor in here isn't?" Violet asked.

"No. Course not. This floor's harder. Hence . . . *mattresses*." Colin made a ta-da kind of gesture, but April was looking at Tim, who caught her gaze. Both of them likely thinking the same thing: that this was also the room with the emergency exit, should they need it. From that room, they could escape into the cellars and the tunnels and hide out—run. If they had to. She just hoped they wouldn't have to.

"Don't you like slumber parties, Vi?" Tim forced a smile, then stepped out into the hall and started dragging in mattress number three.

"This doesn't seem like a slumber party." Violet sounded skeptical. She might have been the youngest and the quietest, but she was no fool.

"Of course it is! Smithers had marshmallows, see?" Colin brandished the bag and two sticks, but Violet just pointed to the corner.

"Then why is Tim hiding a sword underneath that pillow?"

Everyone turned, and Tim froze, and for a second, only the fire made a sound. "I've been practicing a little. I'm not as good as him, but it's better than nothing."

"But why . . ." Sadie trailed off.

Colin rolled his eyes. "Two words, Sade: *masked intruder.* Hasn't it occurred to any of you that this place was thoroughly ransacked and then we walked in before he could finish the job? Doesn't anyone else wonder what he wants? I mean, the art's still on the walls, but he could have been looking for jewelry or bearer bonds or cash or —"

"That's the wrong question," Tim interrupted. Colin looked at him like he was crazy.

"The question isn't what did he want," April explained. "It's did he get it?"

And for a long time they all sat there, half afraid of the answer.

"Maybe the Fake Sentinel got *him*," Violet said, then whispered, "Gabriel."

She shivered and leaned close to April.

"I'm sure that's not it, Vi," Sadie tried. "I'm sure Gabriel's out there looking for this Fake Sentinel — whoever he is. And as soon as Gabriel finds him, he'll come back. I'm sure he'll be back in the morning."

He wasn't back in the morning.

They all sat quietly at the kitchen table, bowls of cereal growing soggy before them.

"We should call someone, right?" Sadie asked. "I think we should call someone."

"No!" Tim snapped.

"But the police need to know. The first forty-eight hours are the most important in any missing persons case, and it's already been . . ." She trailed off and looked at the clock.

"You think he's *missing?*" Tim snapped.

"Uh . . . yes," Sadie said. "What else do you call it when someone disappears without a trace?"

For a moment, Tim just looked at her, as if he couldn't quite believe that someone could be so naive. "I call it *doing a Gabriel Winterborne*."

But Sadie tilted her head and said, "I don't . . ."

"He's done it before, Sade," Colin explained.

"Done what?" Sadie snapped while Colin and Tim shared a skeptical glance.

"Run away," Colin said softly. "This wouldn't be the first time Gabriel has run away."

None of them had known the boy who'd left, but they'd been living with the man who came back for months now, and April couldn't shake the feeling that they didn't know this new Gabriel Winterborne either.

"Gabriel wouldn't leave us." Violet's voice was low but certain. It wasn't a question. It was a fact.

"Exactly!" Sadie cried. "This is his home! And we're—"

"Thorns in his side?" Colin filled in. "A swarm of locusts? Ooh. Wasn't there one last week about boils on his butt? *Butt boils.* That's what he called us, Sade."

Sadie looked down at the table. "He was joking."

He hadn't been joking; April knew it. But she didn't know where he was right that minute, either, and that was the only thing that mattered.

"Gabriel loves us," Violet said, with her big brown eyes looking up at them. She might have been growing like crazy, but she was still just a little girl. Sure, she had no reason to believe that everything would be okay, but she did it anyway.

The look in her eyes, the tone of her voice . . . It broke April's heart. And Tim's too, judging by the look on his face as he shared a glance with Colin. They seemed to be having their own private conversation, but neither said a single word until Colin leaned close and practically whispered, "It's not personal, Vi. It's just . . . Gabriel's not an inside pet. That's all. When you think about it, it's cool he stuck around as long as he did. But he was always gonna run—"

"He didn't run away!" Sadie's chair scraped as it slid back and she jumped to her feet. "No way Gabriel left us. Right? April?"

She looked at April, so certain that she would agree— that it would be the boys against the girls, and the girls had the numbers. But April *wasn't* sure. About anything.

"April?" Sadie asked again, voice cracking.

And April had to admit, "I don't know."

She couldn't look at Sadie. Or at Colin, or Tim, or Violet. She didn't even want to look at herself.

"No, April!" Sadie cried. "You know Gabriel."

"Do I?" April countered. She wanted to laugh. "I mean . . . I don't think he'd *leave us*."

"See?" Sadie sounded vindicated.

"But I never really thought he'd stay."

April let the words hang. She'd never said them out loud, but they'd always been there, deep down. It was what her gut had been telling her all along. "I just don't know."

"Come on, April," Colin started. "You saw him at the gala. He only went to see Izzy, but she wasn't there, and he was miserable. And that was *before* you took your little header onto the stage. He was nine hundred times more comfortable living in a drafty cellar with a bunch of swords than he was at that party. Gabriel Winterborne never wanted to come back. Not really. He met us, and he felt bad and all, so he tried. But he snapped, and . . . he left." Then even Colin had to look away. "Everybody leaves."

April's mom had abandoned her at a fire station when

she was two years old. Colin's mother had shown up at Winterborne House one day, trying to con the world into thinking Colin was Gabriel's son, and then she'd helped herself to the silver and slipped away in the middle of the night, leaving Colin behind. Even Ms. Nelson had walked away, with only a few postcards to show that she remembered they even existed at all.

Everybody left. And Colin and April knew it.

But Sadie's parents had died. Sadie still believed, and so she said, "Gabriel wouldn't run away without telling us!"

"He didn't exactly tell anyone last time," Tim reminded her.

"Last time Evert was trying to kill him!" Sadie snapped.

"What do you think that sword-wielding intruder had planned, Sade? Huh? Whoever he was, he took a little chunk out of Gabriel, remember? But Gabriel didn't call 911. Don't you wonder why that was?"

"Because he's Gabriel, and he's private. Of course he didn't want us to tell anyone about *that,* but—"

"We can't tell anyone about *this.*" Tim cut her off. "We can't tell anyone. Anything."

"He's hurt," Violet said simply. "We're the ones who take care of him when he's hurt."

Violet wasn't wrong, but Tim wasn't in any mood to say so.

"We can't tell anyone he's gone, Vi."

"But—"

"They'd take us!" April snapped, cutting Sadie off. Then she looked at Tim. "That's your point, right? Doesn't matter if Gabriel was kidnapped or ran away or is bleeding out in some ditch somewhere. The short-term results are the same either way, right? We tell someone—*anyone*—he's gone, and Tiny-Pencil Lady comes and we get taken away. That's just math."

"We get taken away *and* split up," Tim added for good measure. Then he looked at Sadie. "Are you willing to risk that?"

"Of course not. It's just . . ." Sadie took a deep breath. "He was bleeding. And hurt. And . . . I don't know. He seemed . . . scared. And I don't think he would have just left us here. Alone. I think something's wrong." She looked at Tim. "Can you say for sure that he's not out there, hurt? Needing us?"

"He might be hurt, Sade. But I'd bet money Gabriel himself would say he doesn't need us," Tim said.

"He'd be wrong," Sadie said.

And April knew that she was right.

April still thought of it as *her* key. She probably always would. She'd worn it around her neck every day for ten long years. It didn't matter that it had Gabriel's family emblem or that it unlocked the secret lair beneath Gabriel's house. Being the Sentinel was Gabriel's family's business. Gabriel's legacy. But the key . . . the key was April's. Even if she did let him borrow it on occasion.

So it felt right in her palm as she crept across the library and toward the big stone fireplace. She pushed the key against the little emblem and twisted, watched the stones fall away. And then she stepped onto the staircase that spiraled into the secret chamber down below.

They'd done a decent job of cleaning the upstairs, but no one had touched the chamber yet. Maybe they were afraid to. The secret lair was like Gabriel himself. It was supposed to be legendary. Invincible. That someone had penetrated the walls of Winterborne House was scary. That whoever it was had made it all the way to this chamber was terrifying.

So April stood on the bottom step for a long time, try-ing to find a pattern in the chaos.

"What do you think he was looking for?"

April jumped at the sound of the voice and turned to see Tim standing on the steps behind her.

"I don't know," she admitted.

The whole house had looked like a bomb had gone off, but this room looked different.

"Nothing's broken," April said once she realized what it was.

"Huh?" Tim asked.

"Upstairs, it's all shattered glass and broken vases and busted-up furniture. But in this room, nothing's actually broken."

"Okay," Tim said slowly.

April was careful as she picked her way through the maze of overturned sparring dummies and the piles of capes and cloaks that had been thrown around the room. The table was covered in giant scrolls of paper and old books and dull knives covered in rust and dust. Dirty dishes that no one had taken upstairs to the kitchen. But still no Gabriel.

Tiny-Pencil Lady's newspaper was still lying on the table where Sadie had left it, and April's picture was staring back at her in black-and-white, so April flipped it over because she already had enough reminders of that night, thank you very much. She didn't need an ego as bruised as the rest of her.

"What are you guys doing down here?" Sadie asked from the stairs. Colin and Violet trailed behind her. "Ooh, what are those?" Sadie made a beeline for the old scrolls because . . . *old scrolls* . . . and Sadie couldn't help herself.

"Maps," Tim said. They shuffled through the stack. "We've got sewer . . . water . . . Looks like they tried to build a subway once upon a time."

"Well, now we know how the Sentinels of yore got around the city undetected," Colin said.

"What's that?" April asked when Violet picked up a leather-bound book and started flipping through the pages.

"Pictures," Violet said. "Look. Gabriel was cute!" She turned the album around, and sure enough, there was a chubby-cheeked baby Gabriel, grinning and covered with drool.

There were handwritten leather-bound journals and an

ornate wooden box full of old compasses. And something that was far more recent.

"That's Izzy's calendar." April froze at the sight.

"What's that doing down here?" Sadie asked, but the answer was obvious.

"Gabriel," April said as Colin picked the book up and began thumbing through the pages. "Gabriel's been looking for Izzy."

"I miss her," Violet said, and April ran a hand through her hair.

"Me too. We need to find her," April said because it seemed like somebody had to.

"He wouldn't want us to tell her he left us," Sadie said.

"I don't care what he wants," Tim snapped. "April's right. Izzy's the only person we can trust not to split us up."

"Yeah. One problem with that," Sadie said. "We have no idea where she is unless that thing happens to say where she was going to be . . . say . . . today?" Sadie sounded hopeful.

Colin opened the book and flipped through the pages. "Ha. Nope. Real exciting stuff here. Let's see . . . Pay taxes.

T'SBD, whatever that is. Foundation meeting, not that she's going to those anymore. Uh . . ." Colin trailed off.

"Well?" Sadie said.

"Dinner with Reggie." He turned the book around so they could see the handwritten inscription. Then he flipped quickly through the pages. "It's in here a few times."

"Reggie, like . . ." Tim prompted.

"The guy at the party," April filled in.

"The one Gabriel pretended not to know," Colin said.

For a moment, Sadie was oddly quiet, then slowly — so slowly that April found it almost painful to watch — she looked down at the newspaper and put a finger on the page. "*This* Reggie Dupree?"

There was no picture, just a headline: MAN INJURED IN FRONT STREET ATTACK.

Sadie started to read, "Mr. Dupree, a resident of the Meridian, was attacked in the early morning hours outside the new luxury high-rise complex. When asked about his attacker, Mr. Dupree laughed and said" — Sadie looked up — "the Sentinel got me."

Colin took the paper from Sadie's limp hands and scanned the article one more time.

"So a crazy guy with swords broke into Winterborne House . . . And then a few hours later, someone attacks Izzy's gentleman friend . . . And at some point, Gabriel disappears . . . So the question is . . . was this"—he pointed at the headline—"the Fake Sentinel?"

"Or the real Gabriel?" April finished.

TWELVE

FRONT STREET

Y ou sure about this?" Colin asked because, really, someone had to. He pulled his navy coat tighter and placed his hands in his pockets and shivered against the frigid wind.

Then he looked up at Tim, who didn't seem the least bit cold, even though he was in the old denim jacket he'd had on all those months ago when he and April and Violet had come to live at Winterborne House. The sleeves were too short now — the coat too tight — almost like he'd outgrown his old life. But he wore it anyway, collar turned up, his own personal suit of armor.

"Do you have any better ideas?" Tim wasn't snapping. He was genuinely open to suggestions, but they'd been over and over their options, and . . . well . . . they didn't have any options. Or no good ones, anyway. So they kept walking. Away from the boat and the docks and down the street that got its name because it ran along in front of the city, skirting the water's edge. There were boulders and docks and stretches of rocky beach on one side, fancy restaurants and shops and cafés where you could sit outside and drink coffee that was too expensive to be called coffee (but was coffee just the same) on the other.

But, eventually, April knew, the pretty buildings with the outdoor tables and white twinkle lights would turn into big, old factories and empty warehouses. Soon, instead of rich ladies carrying tiny dogs in designer purses, there would be alleys full of overflowing dumpsters and cats way too wild to pet. That was the Front Street April had grown up on, but right then, it was several blocks and a million years away from the kids who lived at Winterborne House.

Up ahead, there was a sort of no man's land between those two parts of the city—a place where the street curved farther away from the water's edge and ran up a bit of a ledge, leaving a wide stretch of ground between the city and the sea. It used to be nothing but trash and debris tossed up by the waves, but a tall fence had been erected around it.

"Ooh, that must be where the new park is going," Sadie said, sounding curious.

"And *that* must be where we're heading." Colin pointed to the old factory that stood up ahead, straddling the line between the two versions of Front Street. Beyond that, the buildings were all crumbling bricks and broken glass and rusty metal, but this one had new black trim and a shiny awning and glistening doors that were flanked by two tiny trees covered with twinkle lights even though it wasn't Christmas.

They stopped on the other side of the street, their backs to the tall fence, and studied the building that had been mentioned in the paper.

"The paper said Reggie Dupree has the penthouse," Sadie reminded them, then squinted and stared up. And up. The place was enormous. "So . . . that one?" She pointed to the highest set of windows. There was a huge terrace that overlooked the water and even more tiny Christmas trees.

Colin whistled. "Nice place."

But April was looking at the steep brick walls and the little stickers on all the windows, announcing the name of the best security company in town.

"A little too nice," Tim said as a doorman in a red coat

with shiny gold buttons came out of the building and stood under the awning. "April, any ideas?"

"Usually with these old buildings fire escapes are a good bet, but they've gotten rid of them. Colin, you think we can find . . ."

She looked around, but there were two fewer kids than there should have been.

"Where's Colin?" she asked.

"Where's Violet?" Tim spun and searched the street, but then he stopped. And stared. Because Colin had Violet's hand in his, and they were already talking to the doorman.

"What's he—"

"Wait!" April put her hand on Tim's arm, stopping him. "Let's see . . ."

And then the doorman smiled and held open the door and gestured Colin and Violet inside.

April was sure she didn't stop breathing, but she couldn't say the same for Tim. It seemed to take forever for the access door on the side of the building to swing open and for Violet to pop out and give the universal gesture for *don't just stand there, come on already.*

In a flash, Sadie, and Tim, and April were running

across the street and through the door and into a stairwell where every little whisper echoed off the metal stairs and concrete walls, but that didn't stop Tim from snapping, "What did you do?"

"I got us in." Colin wiggled an eyebrow, looking smug.

"How?" Sadie asked in her scientist voice. April could practically see gears turning in her brain. Soon she was going to start talking about sample sizes and standard deviations and how many times they'd have to duplicate it and whether or not they should account for the weather and the day of the week.

But Colin just threw out his arms. "You don't get it, do you? We're the rich kids now! Rich kids don't ask to be let into the fancy apartment building. Rich kids walk up to the doorman who still has the tag on his jacket and ask if their Uncle Reggie's package is here yet."

Then he waggled a package in Tim's face just for good measure.

"What if he wasn't expecting a package?" Sadie asked, but Colin simply rolled his eyes.

"Anyone who lives in a building like this is *always* expecting a package." He put a foot on the bottom stair. "Come on."

And then they climbed.

Up and up and up, footsteps echoing on metal steps.

"Maybe. Next time," Sadie huffed, "We. Can. Investigate. Someone. On a. Lower. Floor."

But eventually they pushed out into a wide, bright foyer. There was an elevator and a skylight overhead, an orchid on a big, round table. And a glossy set of double doors that didn't even have a number.

"So." It was Tim's turn to sound smug. "What's your plan now?"

But Colin wasn't worried. Colin simply . . . knocked.

"No!" April snapped. Sadie started looking for a place to hide. Tim looked ready to grab Violet and run down the stairs as fast as he could, but nothing happened, and the door stayed closed.

"Oh." Colin sounded sad and more than a little disappointed. He looked down at the package in his hand like it wasn't the gift he'd been hoping for.

"Great plan," Tim snapped. "What were you gonna do? Just ask him?"

But before Colin could answer, a voice came from behind them, saying, "Ask me what?"

THIRTEEN

TAKING CANDY FROM STRANGERS

April had seen Reggie Dupree once before, but something about the man was . . . different. Maybe it was the fact that he'd traded his tuxedo for a hoodie, but he seemed more human somehow. Or maybe that was because he had a black eye and a cut on his jaw and his left arm was in a sling. Plus, as he stood outside the elevator of his fancy apartment, he seemed more than a little confused.

"Can I help you?" he asked Colin, who snapped back into con mode and grinned up at the stranger.

"I'm sorry, Mr. Dupree. I think I got your package by mistake." Colin held up the package, and Reggie took it.

"Thanks! But I was kind of hoping . . ." He looked at April, Sadie, and Violet. "Are you Girl Scouts?" Wordlessly, they shook their heads. "Darn it. Do you know any Girl Scouts? I could really go for some cookies."

April wasn't expecting Sadie to admit, "No. I got kicked out."

The man laughed like he didn't know if she was being serious, because . . . well . . . he didn't know Sadie. "Wait. For real? You got kicked out of the Girl Scouts?" he asked, and Sadie grimaced.

"There was a *badge incident*. I don't like to talk about it." Sadie still sounded bitter, and April was almost afraid to ask for details.

Luckily, Reggie picked that moment to reach for his keys. With the package tucked under one arm and the sling on the other, he fumbled a little. Then he winced.

"Are you okay?" Colin asked. "We read about what happened."

It seemed like they all held their breaths as the man looked down at the sling, as if he'd already forgotten the story. Or maybe like he wanted to. "This?" he asked. Then he shrugged. "This is just doctors covering their . . . *rear ends*," he said in the way adults always do when they remember they're talking to children.

He looked at Violet and Sadie, Colin and Tim, but

when he saw April, he hesitated. He looked at her like Sadie looked at math.

Then he glanced back at the package. "Thanks for dropping this by. It must have been a lot of trouble."

"No trouble at all!" Colin said.

"I don't know about that," the stranger said. "You're a long way from Winterborne House."

At first, April felt shocked. "How did you—" she started.

"You mean other than the crest on your clothes?" Then April felt stupid. "I read the paper, too. It's not a great picture, but it left an impression. Man, now I want cookies, and it's all your fault. Do you guys want cookies? 'Cause there's a place up the block . . ." He slipped his keys back in his pocket and dropped the package on the table with the orchid and pushed the button for the elevator.

Then he looked down at April. "That looked like quite a fall. Are you okay? You weren't hurt?"

And April realized that no one had asked her that before. She also realized, "I'm pretty good at falling. I've had a lot of practice."

The man laughed, then gestured to his injured arm. "Me too."

When they reached the lobby, he waved at the doorman and pulled on a pair of sunglasses before stepping out into the windy day.

"Come on," he said, then gestured toward a store with a fancy sign that read **CANDY'S SWEETSHOP**.

"Reggie!" the girl behind the counter called over the dinging of the little bell as the door swung open. "The usual?"

"Yeah. And whatever these guys want."

Everybody froze. And stared. Their jaws must have been hanging open or something, because he looked confused. "What is it? What's wrong?"

"Nothing," April said, stealing a glance at Tim and Violet. "I just . . . uh . . . I don't think we've ever been here before." She didn't think. She knew. Because Tim and Violet and April had been locked inside the system and Sadie and Colin had been locked inside of Winterborne House and not even the box labeled **SMITHERS'S EMERGENCY CHOCOLATE** could have prepared them for a place like that.

The store looked like something from a movie, with glass jars brimming with candy and cases full of chocolate and, behind the counter, row after row of cookies. Every kind you could dream of and a few more April never even knew were possible.

"Ahh," Reggie said, and April could tell that he'd remembered. Who they were. Where they were from. That they might live in a mansion but they were one bad mistake (or missing guardian) from the other end of Front Street. "You know, I've got an idea. Hey, Candy!" he called, and all of the kids looked at him like he was crazy. "That's her name." He pointed at the woman behind the counter. "Candy. And she runs a sweetshop, isn't that amazing?" Then he turned back to the woman. "We're gonna need a sampler."

Turns out, "sampler" is *rich person* for "one of everything." Five minutes later, they were sitting at a table with cookies and chocolates and gummy worms and gummy bears and even gummy Sentinels. April eyed it all like she didn't know where to start. Probably because she didn't know where to start.

"Do you like toffee?" Reggie said softly when she'd sat there a little too long, staring.

She felt her eyes get big. "It's my favorite."

"Cool! Mine too. Here. You have this." He slid a package in front of her.

"But it's your usual."

"Nah." He smiled. "I can have it anytime."

She heard what he didn't say: that she couldn't. Gabriel could have bought them all the candy in the universe, but candy was never, ever on the list.

"Do you have kids?" Violet asked, which was strange. Violet never talked to strangers.

It took a moment for Mr. Dupree to say, "I did."

Maybe it was the past tense verb, but April knew there was a story there. And she knew it was a sad one. But Violet didn't know.

She asked, "What happened?"

"Vi—" Tim shook his head real quick, but Mr. Dupree said, "It's okay. It was a long time ago."

"I'm sorry," April said, because she was pretty sure that was what she was supposed to say, and she didn't ask a single question because there are some scabs you should never, ever pick at.

"So how do you know Izzy?" she asked instead, because that should have been a happy topic.

"The park," he said, even though he'd just shoved half a cookie in his mouth.

"You met at the park?" Sadie asked.

"No. The new park—down by the water. We're both on the planning committee. It'll be so cool once it's finished. We're gonna have it all. Skateboard ramp thingies and jungle gyms and a big climbing wall and one of those"—he made a kind of crazy motion with his hands—"you know, with the water?"

"Splashpad?" Sadie guessed.

Reggie snapped his fingers. "Yes! Thank you! It'll be awesome. Eventually. Now it's just really expensive mud."

"Have you heard from Izzy lately?" Sadie asked.

"No. I haven't talked to her."

"She's . . . uh . . . not with the foundation anymore," Colin told him.

"Ahhh," he said slowly, studying them all in turn. "Something tells me the . . . uh . . . *foundation* would like her back." (He wasn't talking about the foundation.) "I can see why." He took a deep breath. "She's really great."

"She's the best," Tim said.

"Is that why you're here? Because you're looking for Izzy?"

It was as good a reason as any, so they all nodded yes.

"We miss her," Violet added, and for a moment they all sat in somber silence.

Only Sadie was brave enough to break it. "Uh . . . Mr. Dupree?"

"Mr. Dupree? Nobody calls me that."

"Isn't that your name?" Sadie asked, confused.

"Well, technically, my name is Reginald William Alister Claudius Brian Dupree."

"Wow," Colin mumbled.

"The second," Reggie added. "So, yeah. Call me Reggie."

"Uh . . . Reggie, what, uh, happened?" She didn't say more. She just gestured at his sling and let the silence do the rest.

"This? It's nothing." (It wasn't nothing.) "I'm fine!" (He wasn't fine.)

So April asked, "What happened? You can tell us." (He probably shouldn't have told them.)

But he looked at them all in turn, like he was weighing his words and trying to make them balance. "No. You guys wouldn't believe me."

"Try us," Tim said. There was a hard gleam in his eyes. It was almost a challenge. A dare.

So Reggie took a deep breath and said, "After the gala, I thought, hey, it's not that far . . . It's a nice night . . . I can walk." He blushed. "Turns out, I shouldn't have walked. Someone jumped me. I mean, like, literally *jumped*. Like, off a building or something. One moment I was walking along, and the next I was on the ground. I must have landed wonky, because this" — he held out the arm in the sling — "happened. I didn't realize it until I tried to fight, but my wrist was already, like, five times bigger than it should have been, and I kind of wanted to . . . you know . . . puke." He looked green with the memory. "And I must have hit my head or something, because for a second there, I could have sworn . . ."

Then he seemed to remember who he was talking to. He closed his mouth like he'd already said too much.

"What?" April leaned forward and fiddled with the straw in her water glass. "You could have sworn . . ."

He looked guilty. And foolish. Like this was his deepest, darkest secret but he was dying to tell someone. "I could have sworn it was the Sentinel. I mean it was all there. Hat. Swords. Cape. You know . . . *the Sentinel*. But that's crazy. I mean, every third guy at the gala was dressed like that. I probably just had it on my mind and then I hit my head and my brain filled in the blanks."

"But did he look like any particular Sentinel?" Colin

nudged, and April held her breath, waiting for him to say, *Yeah, actually, he looked like Gabriel Winterborne!* But Reggie shook his head.

"Don't all Sentinels look alike?"

"What did he want?" Tim asked.

Reggie shrugged. "Usual stuff, I guess. Wallet. Phone. Which is a bummer. I had a bunch of work stuff on there."

"Did you see a face?" Tim asked. "Hear a voice? Did you see where he came from? Where he went?"

"No. I was kinda out of it. Look, you guys don't need to be afraid. Trust me. No one is breaking into Winterborne House."

He actually laughed. Because he thought they were just kids and Winterborne House was just a mansion. He didn't know that sword-wielding madmen were a standard part of the Winterborne package.

When his laughter faded and they were all back in that place of awkward silence, he fingered the empty wrappers on the table and said, "So . . . uh . . . Gabriel? What's his deal?"

April was just starting to think about what she should —and shouldn't—tell him when a small voice piped up, saying, "He's in love with Izzy."

"Vi—" Tim tried, but Violet talked on.

"And Izzy's in love with him. And when she gets back, she's going to marry Gabriel, and we're going to be a family." Violet grinned, her mouth covered with chocolate.

She sounded like April used to sound—so sure her mother would come back for her. So certain that she'd get a happy ending. But April's mother wasn't coming back. April's mother was probably dead. Gabriel might be dead. And suddenly April's stomach hurt in a way that had nothing to do with eating too much candy.

"You okay there, April?" Reggie asked as Tim and Sadie boxed up all the leftovers.

"Yeah."

"Do you guys need a ride home?"

"No," April said too quickly. "I mean . . . we've got a ride."

"Do you need something else?" He wasn't talking about chocolate or cookies or anything with *gummy* in the name. "If you do . . . you can call my building. They can get a message to me anytime. If you need help. Or something."

But April . . . All April wanted was Gabriel.

FOURTEEN

A DOG THAT LOOKS LIKE A FOX

The sun was still up when they said goodbye to Reggie Dupree outside those big, glossy doors, not far from the doorman in the burgundy blazer. But it was getting later. The wind was cooler, and maybe it was her belly full of sugar, but April was very, very ready to go home.

"This way," Tim said.

"But—" Sadie pointed toward downtown and the dock and the boat and even Winterborne House itself.

"I need to talk to someone," Tim explained.

"Who?" Sadie asked.

"Someone who might have seen something."

"The article said there weren't any witnesses," Sadie

reminded him, but Tim actually laughed. Sadie looked hurt.

"The article said the *police* said there weren't any witnesses," he told her.

"I know. That's what I said."

But then Tim grew serious. "It's Front Street, Sadie. There are never any witnesses on Front Street. At least none who are willing to talk to the police."

Then Tim headed to the other end of Front Street, and the rest of them followed. With every step, the wind blew colder and the sun crept lower. A piece of newspaper blew along a dingy sidewalk.

"Maybe we should come back in the morning?" Sadie asked, but Tim kept walking.

"Front Street doesn't do mornings," he said.

"But—"

"Look, Sade." Tim stopped and turned on her—on all of them. "See that window? That's Crazy Pete's place. But Crazy Pete's name is Larry. See that dry cleaner's?" He pointed at a dirty window with a half-burned-out neon sign announcing that everything was half price on Tuesday. "The only thing they launder in there is money. See her?"

This time, Tim pointed at an old woman with long white braids and an even longer skirt. Colin was creeping closer and looking at the things the woman had laid out for sale atop a folding table, but Tim wasn't watching, even as he said, "In about five seconds, her skirt is gonna start barking, and then Colin's gonna get attacked by a dog that—"

"Looks like a fox," April said, the words almost like something from a dream. Or maybe just another life. Then, almost on cue, the skirt started barking and Colin leapt back as the tiny, fox-shaped head peeked out from beneath the heavy fabric.

Sadie looked at Tim like he was psychic.

"You know how, in your lab, things make sense because it's science and science has rules?" he asked her.

"Yeah."

"Well." Tim shoved his hands in the pockets of the jacket that didn't quite fit anymore and looked around the neighborhood that didn't quite fit either. "Front Street is my lab, Sade. And it has rules too. You can go back to the boat, though, if you want to. I just need to see her first."

"Who?" Sadie asked.

He pointed at the old woman. "Her."

"You've been gone a long time, child," the old woman called as they got closer. "Thought you forgot about us."

"Never, Madge." Tim leaned down, and the dog ran to lick his fingers that probably tasted like candy.

"Don't you spoil my dog," the old woman snapped, but she was smiling.

He looked up at her and grinned. "Maybe I'll spoil you?" he said, then gave her their bag of leftovers.

Sadie looked like she wanted to protest, but April elbowed her, and Colin just looked bewildered.

"Is Tim being charming? It seems like Tim's being charming. Charming is *my* thing."

"You charmer," the old woman told Tim, and Colin gasped.

"See?"

"Shhh," Sadie said, easing closer.

"Where you been, Timmy? Haven't seen you around," the old woman said.

"New house. It's outside town a little. Haven't been back this way in a while."

Then Madge gave them all a good look. "I see."

"How you been?" Tim asked.

But the woman looked him in the eye and said, "Why don't you ask me what you really want to know?"

Tim ran one shoe through a line of dirt in the gutter. "Saw something in the paper about someone getting mugged around here a couple nights ago. You know anything about that?"

She looked at him for a long time. "You believe in ghost stories now, Timmy?"

"Just curious," Tim said. "I figured if anyone knew whether the Sentinel was real or not, it'd be you."

"The Sentinel's always been a legend." The old woman looked at April. "Doesn't mean he isn't real."

"And the other night . . ." April couldn't help but inch forward "Was that the real Sentinel?"

"Never saw one bleed before," the old woman said.

"He got hurt?" April asked. "During the fight?"

"Oh, he was hurt, all right. But he was that way when he got here."

"Excuse me." Sadie pushed forward. "Can you point us to where the attack happened? And at approximately what time? And do you know of any security cameras that had a good view of the area? Maybe—"

But the old woman looked at Tim like Sadie wasn't speaking at all. "You're in a good place, Timmy. You ought to stay there. Now go on. Get out of here. Front Street's no place for you lot." She looked into the distance. "Front Street's no place for anyone."

And then Tim turned and walked away.

"Tim," Sadie said, trying to stop him. "Wait. She didn't answer your questions."

"Yes. She did."

"No." Sadie sounded confused. "She—"

"She said whoever attacked Reggie wasn't hurt *in* the fight, Sade," Tim snapped. "She said he was hurt when he got here. So she told us, okay? She told us it was Gabriel."

FIFTEEN

THE PLAYGROUND

On the long walk back to the boat, the world felt darker than it should have. Sadie would have said it was because of the tilt of the earth and the position of the sun, but April knew it was more than that. She knew in her gut that it didn't matter what the clock said, the light would have gone out after that, no matter what.

Gabriel was hurt. Gabriel was out there. And it seemed more certain than ever that he wasn't coming home.

"I don't get it," Sadie said softly. "It doesn't make sense. What was Gabriel doing down here? What does he want with Reggie?"

"I don't know, Sade."

"Why hasn't he come home?" Sadie's voice cracked. It sounded like April's heart felt.

Somewhere, a dog barked. Streetlights flickered off and on, and even the shadows seemed to move, blown with the trash by the breeze. Something darted across the street in front of them. Behind them, glass shattered, like a bottle tossed to the gutter.

"Who's there?" Colin called.

But then there was a hiss and a cat jumped off of an overflowing dumpster, and April felt herself start to breathe again.

Then, at the end of the block, a streetlight flickered off. Then on. And for a second, April thought it was a trick of the light—a fantasy. A ghost. But as the light grew brighter, she saw the cape. And the hat. And two very shiny swords.

"Is that . . ." Violet started.

"That's not Gabriel," Colin said, and even though April really, really wanted him to be wrong, she knew in her heart he was right.

"Move!" she snapped, and they took off, darting down a side street, but they had to freeze when a man appeared at the end of the block.

"Back up," Tim whispered, but two more men were already behind them, talking and laughing until they noticed the kids, and then they weren't laughing anymore.

"Well, what do we have here?" one of the men asked in a way that made the little hairs on the back of April's neck stand up.

"This way!" Tim pushed Violet toward an alley so small that April hadn't even known it was there, and then they were off, running through a warren of twisty streets and filthy alleys that should have been too narrow — too dark — but Tim knew them like the back of his hand, and he didn't slow down. They just kept running and dodging and weaving until they were shooting out onto Front Street.

Tim grabbed Violet's hand. "We're okay now. No one's following us. See?" But when he looked back, April noticed, he didn't seem any less worried. "We'll get to the boat soon."

"Maybe we should go to Reggie's?" Sadie asked.

"No," Tim snapped.

"But—"

"Gabriel didn't trust that guy," Tim said.

"Gabriel's gone, mate."

"He was a friend of Izzy's," Violet pointed out.

"No," April said. "Tim's right. We have to go home." Because she finally had a home, and she wasn't going to leave it, not for all the candy in the world.

"But—"

"Gabriel would never hurt us, but he did hurt Reggie, which means Reggie can't be trusted," April snapped. "That's just math."

"When this is all over, we're gonna have a long talk about what math is," Sadie said, but April walked faster. She could see Reggie's building in the distance, bright lights like a beacon. The marina would be a little farther down. And their boat. And home. They just had to keep walking. They just had to—

"Hello there."

April hadn't seen the man jump out of the shadows—not until it was way too late. His arms were already around her, squeezing so tight she couldn't breathe. And his breath was warm on her ear as he whispered, "You can run, but you can't—Oomph!"

That was when Violet kicked him. Hard.

"April!" Sadie screamed, while Tim and Colin lunged,

knocking April and the man to the ground. As soon as they struck the pavement, the man lost his grip and April rolled free. She jumped to her feet and yelled, "Run!"

That time of night, there wasn't much traffic on Front Street, so it wasn't hard to dodge the cars as they ran to the sidewalk on the other side, where a tall chain link fence separated the street from the water.

They just had to get to the boat . . . They just had to get out onto the water . . . They just had to—

There was a squeal of tires as another man jumped out of the street and onto the sidewalk in front of them, cutting them off.

"Not so fast," he said while the first man caught up and flanked them from behind.

They were hemmed in. Again.

"Come on, now. No one has to get hurt." The man's voice was menacing and cold, but he didn't sound like Front Street looked. His accent was too polished, and his clothes were too clean and new. He didn't fit in. He didn't make sense. Nothing made sense! But it didn't have to. It didn't change the fact that the men were inching closer and the kids were shrinking back, pressing against the cold metal fence.

"Anyone have any ideas?" Tim asked.

"Pray?" April said, and it must have worked because, just then, the streetlight overhead exploded in a burst of sparks and fire.

"Here!" Colin shouted, and April saw him prying back a tiny gap in the fence. It was just big enough for April to squeeze through, and she didn't stop and think as she crawled into the darkness.

She felt Sadie and Tim and Violet at her back. She heard Sadie shout, "Colin, come on!"

Colin's head peeked through, but the rest of him didn't follow. He kept kicking, windmilling, like a car stuck in the mud, and April realized a hand had the back of his coat and it wasn't letting go.

"Here!" she shouted, then started undoing Colin's buttons.

"Hurry up, love," he said.

"Go!" she said, and then he wiggled free. Instantly, there was a thud on the other side of the fence as the man holding the coat fell back, but that wasn't April's problem.

No. April's problem was broader. And taller. And seemed infinitely darker as she stared up at a mountain of gravel that blocked the kids in close to the fence. She couldn't see the water. She couldn't see . . . anything. Just an endless wall of black.

"Where do we go?" April asked.

Behind them, there was cursing. The fence rattled and shook as the big men tried to fit through the tiny hole.

"Over!" Tim shouted, and then they started to climb.

But the pile was so steep, and the gravel was so loose that, for every three steps April took, she ended up sliding two steps back down. They couldn't stick together because the rocks simply couldn't hold them all and they kept slipping and sliding, begging for purchase.

"Spread out!" Sadie called, so they stretched across the massive pile and started to climb. Eventually, April reached the summit of Mount Gravel and looked out across the park that wasn't a park just yet.

In the moonlight, she could just make out piles of lumber and supplies, bulldozers and backhoes. A half-finished playground with forts and towers, monkey bars and swings that seemed to morph and change as the moon played peekaboo behind a layer of thick clouds.

It was almost beautiful. Almost peaceful. But then there was a noise behind them, the crashing of the fence, and April whirled to see the men pushing their way inside.

Which was a mistake, because, turns out, whirling is an excellent way to turn a gravel mountain into a gravel avalanche.

"Ooh!" April screamed as her feet flew out from under her and she landed on her butt and started to slide. Faster and faster, all the way to the bottom, where she landed with a crash.

And judging by the screams around her, she wasn't the only one.

"April, where are—" Sadie started, but the cursing of the men cut her off.

"Run!" April yelled, and she heard them all take off, gravel flying beneath their feet as they spread out, heading in different directions.

April couldn't see Tim or Violet or Sadie. She was aware, faintly, of Colin running along in her wake, following her through the maze of heavy equipment and stacks of supplies. When they reached a huge metal tube, April ducked down and darted inside, but she kept running.

April had learned a long time ago to always keep running.

She stayed low in the tube and stepped softly, but then there was a flash of movement at the other end, and she froze. She almost fell when Colin ran into her back, but neither said a word as they watched a figure creep across the mouth of the tube, then peer inside, searching the darkness while April stood as quiet and as still as the grave until the man stepped back and turned away.

"It's too dark," Colin whispered. "He can't see us. Come on." Then they eased back the way they'd come, as quickly and quietly as they could.

And then they were out in the night air again. Thankfully, it was impossible to get turned around, not with the inky black ocean on one side and the lights of the city on the other, so she and Colin didn't even have to debate which way to go. They had to get out of the unfinished park. They had to get to their boat. They had to get home. At least while they still had one.

But a noise on the water made April stagger to a stop.

"What was—" A bright light came from the water, slicing through the darkness like a blade, sweeping over everything—searching—and when it landed on April, it burned.

April threw an arm across her eyes and squinted against the glare. The light was too bright, and she knew that they were sitting ducks there, caught in the spotlight's glare with nowhere to run or hide. It was just a matter of time until—

"Over there!" the British man shouted, and April spun to see him pointing at them from atop a stack of boulders. He leapt to the ground and strolled toward them, but then he just . . . fell down? Which seemed too lucky to be true, and when April saw the dark figure behind him, she knew it wasn't luck at all.

"Gabriel?" April didn't mean to shout, but hope was already swelling in her chest. She wanted to scream with relief and cry with joy. She wanted to believe that it was him. That he was back. That he would always find her, come for her, save her.

April wasn't thinking then. She was running through the beam of the spotlight and toward the figure in the shadows. But someone caught her hand.

"April!" Colin shouted, pulling her back. "Still not Gabriel!"

For a second, it was like a dream—or maybe a nightmare—as the bright beam of light shifted away from April and Colin and onto the figure all in black. It seemed too bright as it reflected off the shiny swords, and April felt almost cold without its heat, but there was no denying that she wasn't in the spotlight anymore.

"April, we have to go." Colin tugged on her hand. "Now!"

But April couldn't budge, because one of the men had already leapt off a pile of lumber and landed on the Fake Sentinel. They crashed too hard to the ground, but the Fake Sentinel rolled and bounced back, then stopped . . . And looked at April and Colin and yelled, "Run!"

And April stopped thinking. She stopped feeling—not hope or fear or anger. April didn't even feel the cold as she and Colin shot off across the uneven ground, dodging behind stacks and piles, leaping over huge beams and ditches full of water.

April didn't have time to think about what she'd seen. She didn't dare stop to think about what it meant.

She just knew they had to get out of there. And they had to hide. *Both*. But they couldn't do both. They couldn't unless . . .

April looked up.

Huge wooden pillars were set into the ground, rising high into the air, holding up slides and ropes and monkey bars. It was a place built for play. But April didn't play. April survived. And lately survival was a full-time job.

She glanced at Colin, who must have been thinking the exact same thing because they both bolted to the huge wall covered with handholds and footholds and, together, began to climb.

Once they reached the top, it was easy to move across the huge platforms made to look like an ancient castle, over monkey bars that stretched out into the night. But at the sound of a noise from down below, they froze. April didn't dare move, even though the cold monkey bars were too hard on her bony knees and something metal was sticking up, gouging April's palm, so sharp she knew she might be bleeding.

"They're around here somewhere," a voice said.

In front of her, Colin whirled his head around and looked at her, and she knew exactly what he was thinking: *They're right below us!*

If the men looked up . . . If the boat swung the light that way . . . There were a dozen ways things could get worse because, in April's experience, things can always get worse. It was up to her to make them better.

But she had sore knees, a stomach that felt weird from too much sugar and adrenaline, and a giant bolt cutting into her hand, so . . .

April picked up the bolt.

And threw it into the darkness, where it pinged off some rocks.

"What was that?" one of the men asked. When they moved to go investigate, April and Colin took a risk and crawled faster.

But then the spotlight hit them, and April froze in the glare.

"Up there!" the men shouted, then bolted toward the jungle gym and started to climb.

But there was an advantage to (1) a bright light and (2) being seen: April and Colin didn't have to be slow and quiet anymore. They could be as loud as they wanted as long as they were fast. As long as they were smart. So they rushed across the monkey bars and over the next platform.

"That way!" Colin pointed when two paths branched off of the platform, and they took off in the direction that pointed toward the city and the docks and their way home.

And they ran faster.

Right up until the point when they jolted to a stop.

"So . . . this is still under construction," Colin said as they looked down at the thirty-foot drop to the hard ground below.

Behind them, the men were coming. April had lost the shadows and the element of surprise. She'd lost everything but her nerve.

Because nerve was the only thing that April had always had plenty of.

Overhead, there was a pulley with a rope that ran down to the ground where it wrapped around one of the huge wooden beams. April had lived with Sadie long enough to know what it was all for. And she'd lived alone long enough to have the guts to do it.

"Colin?" She looked at him, the unasked question in her eyes.

He nodded. "On three."

The man lunged, and April yelled, "Three!" and then they ran together, reaching out and jumping, grabbing the rope. She felt a surge and sudden stop when their weight countered the mass of the beam on the ground. And when the giant piece of wood started to rise and they started to fall, April felt weightless. April could fly.

It was almost a disappointment to finally touch the

ground, but April couldn't think about that. She could only run, heading for the lights of the city and the edge of the park. They were so close to the streets and, in April's mind, freedom.

They were going to make it, April thought, until a third man stepped out of the shadows, blocking their path, nothing but a silhouette against the glare of the spotlight, and April felt the world closing in like the darkness that lived just outside that too-bright beam of light.

"It doesn't have to be this hard," the man said.

"Okay," April told him. "We should make it harder."

She looked at Colin, who said, "Two of us. One of him."

That's just math, April thought, then took off in one direction. She heard Colin running in another. But the spotlight stayed trained on April, almost hot in the cold air. But at least she could see enough that she didn't fall over the big boxes labeled **DANGER: EXPLOSIVES**. She could recognize the sound of feet running behind her, too heavy to belong to her friends.

They were out there somewhere, lost in the darkness and the shadows. Safe? April hoped they were safe.

Something told her that they'd be okay as long as the spotlight and the men kept following April, so she headed for the big boulders that bordered the water. She tried not to think about the shouts behind her—the men who were closing in.

She scampered over the slick rocks and rough ground. She climbed. She clawed. And when a hand reached out and grabbed her ankle, she kicked.

"Get back—"

But before the man could finish, she saw the flicker of light off of two shiny blades, and in that moment, April believed in the Sentinel—not the Winterborne family secret. She believed in ghosts and legends, in supernatural vigilantes and ancient beings meant to keep stupid kids safe from their own foolishness.

The only thing she knew for sure was that it wasn't Gabriel. Because Gabriel had left them. Gabriel was gone. Gabriel might have been hurt or trapped or on the other side of the earth right then, but the person who had driven him from his own home was there, fighting for the kids he had abandoned.

But there were too many men. The rocks were too

slick. One moment, April was looking at the bright flashes of moonlight on steel, and the next, the Fake Sentinel was falling off of the rocks and into the sea.

The men stood there for a moment, not sure how they got so lucky.

And then they remembered April, who had finally made it to the wooden pier that ran from the street out into the inky black water.

Her friends felt a million miles away, so it was strange to hear her name on the air.

"April!" someone shouted, and she looked up to see a shiny car sitting on the street at the end of the pier. Reggie Dupree was leaning over the front seat, yelling through the passenger side window. "April, come on!"

April froze.

Her options were clear:

She could get in the car with Ms. Nelson's friend—the goofy guy who liked cookies and candy.

Or she could stay there and let unknown goons drag her to an unknown place for unknown reasons.

Suddenly a massive boom rang out. The pier shook. The men actually ducked as fire filled the sky over the park.

"What was that?" one of them yelled.

But April just smiled and said, "Sadie found the explosives."

And then she turned and ran as hard and as fast as she could, away from the rocks and the fire and the man in the car idling at the curb. April ran away from all of it.

Sirens sounded in the distance. Soon the park and the harbor would be a swirl of spinning lights, but April was already jumping as far as she could, out into the dark, vast water of the sea.

SIXTEEN

THE GIRL WHO JUMPED INTO THE SEA

The first thing April felt was the cold. The bone-chilling, mind-numbing pressure that surrounded her until she thought her lungs might burst.

The second thing she felt was an overwhelming sense of déjà vu. Maybe it had all been a dream. Maybe she was still adrift on the waves outside Uncle Evert's mini mansion, looking for Gabriel Winterborne. Maybe the last few months hadn't happened at all.

But there had been no smoke the last time. No sirens. No shouts. She'd been alone in the darkness then, searching. And this time she was desperate not to be found.

So she didn't call out. She didn't even know who to call for. She just floated on the waves until the current carried her farther from the park and the fire and the swirling lights. Black smoke blocked out the moon, as the sirens got closer and closer. Soon she'd be able to see swirling red lights and hear the cries of firefighters and cops. Television helicopters wouldn't be far behind.

She remembered a distant cry of "Fall back!" and the roar of the boat with the searchlight speeding away, so April knew the men were gone, but April was anything but safe, because the cold . . . the cold was almost too much. Her teeth chattered, and she couldn't feel her fingers.

"April!" someone shouted from the rocks. "April!"

She used to have a friend who sounded like that.

She used to have a friend.

No. *Friends.* April used to have four friends. She was just trying to remember their names when something latched on to her coat and towed her to shore.

Hands slapped her face, and her skin was so cold it felt brittle — like it might shatter.

"Easy, Sade," Colin said.

"April," Sadie was saying. "April, wake up. Can you —"

"The Sentinel!" April said, bolting upright. "We have to find —"

"Looking for this?" That's when April noticed Tim's jeans were soaked from the knees down and, at his feet, lay a figure in black, unmoving on the ground. She couldn't see what was wrong, not with all the dark clothes and deep shadows, but the Fake Sentinel looked smaller, frailer.

"Who is he?" she asked, looking from the figure on the ground to the mask in Sadie's hands. "Who is he!" she shouted, but Sadie just shook her head.

"He's . . . a she."

And that's when she saw the face that was beautiful even underneath a mask of bruises.

"April . . ." the woman said, twisting and writhing in pain. "Help April."

"April's here," Sadie said.

"Not safe. She's not safe. She's not . . . "

"Why isn't April safe?" Sadie asked.

But then the eyes flew open. It must have taken all the woman's strength to choke out a cold, hard laugh before saying, "Because I'm her mother."

And then she passed out cold.

April didn't think about the words. She must have heard

them wrong. After all, there was a sound like a freight train suddenly booming in her ears. She was wrong. She was wrong. She was wrong. She had to be!

But when she looked at Tim, he just shrugged and said, "Sadie, we're gonna have to move another body."

SEVENTEEN

THE MINI MANSION. AGAIN.

The closer they got to Winterborne House, the more the wind seemed to blow. Colder. And Harder. Like the sea was trying to push them back — like maybe it knew something they didn't. Like maybe they should "do a Gabriel Winterborne," as Colin had put it. Like maybe they should just drift away.

But then they'd never get Gabriel back. And they just *had* to get Gabriel back! Gabriel would know what the truth was. He'd know what to do. He might yell and scream and use all his favorite Portuguese swear words, but he'd know. And then April could stop thinking. Because April was so tired of thinking. And shaking. She couldn't stop. And she wasn't entirely sure it had anything to do with the cold.

Winterborne House was shining like a beacon, far off in the distance, when the boat began to slow.

"What are you doing?" Sadie was leaning over the woman who lay on the bottom of the boat beneath a mountain of blankets, but she looked up. "Tim? Why are you slowing down? We've got to get her back to—"

"We can't go to Winterborne House, Sade," Colin told her, but she cut her eyes back to Tim.

"Of course we can. We *live* at Winterborne House." Sadie sounded confused. "If we don't take her to Winterborne House, where can we . . ."

But Sadie trailed off as a smaller building came into view.

The first time April had ever seen Evil Uncle Evert's house, she'd thought it was exactly like Winterborne House, only smaller, but that night it looked downright ominous, standing at the top of the steep cliffs, not a single light burning in a single window.

"The mini mansion. But why . . ."

"They want me," April said. "Or her? Whoever *they* are, they want . . . us?" No one had wanted April for ten long years, and now it felt like everybody did, and April didn't like it one bit. Besides, it didn't change the facts.

"I lost my coat, Sade," Colin explained. "So even if they didn't know where we live before, they will now. We can't go back to Winterborne House."

"But Gabriel's going to be scared when he gets back and we're not there," Violet said.

April and Tim and Colin shared a look, but no one said what they were thinking: that Gabriel might not be coming back.

"The mini mansion's close enough that we can keep an eye out for Gabriel if we need to, Vi," Colin told her. "And we gotta get April and her mom——"

"She's not my mom," April said.

"But——" Colin began.

"I don't care what she said," April snapped. "That woman is not my mother." Her voice quivered, and it took all her strength to finish, "I don't have a mother."

"April, you're shaking," Tim said.

"No. I'm . . . fine." Her teeth rattled together.

"You're not fine. We've got to get you inside." Tim steered the boat into a small cove that was largely hidden from the open water. From there, April could look straight up at the long, steep staircase that rose along the face of the cliffs, higher and higher.

"Um . . . how are we gonna do that exactly?" Colin asked. He looked from the unconscious woman to the twisty stairs.

Sadie beamed. "Just leave that to me."

"You think we can do this?" Tim asked twenty minutes later as they dragged the woman's still unconscious body out of the boat.

"Sure. She's lighter than Gabriel, and we hoisted him up . . ." But April trailed off as Tim cocked an eyebrow. "You weren't talking about body moving, were you?"

Before Tim could answer, a voice shouted down from overhead. "Look out below!" And a rope fell from the sky, unfurling before them.

It was a little surreal to see an unconscious woman rise into the air like a kite on the wind. April half suspected they could have made her dance like a puppet if they'd wanted. It made April nostalgic for a simpler time when they only had to deal with one sword-wielding vigilante, but those days were over and they weren't coming back again anytime soon.

By the time they reached the big stone patio, April couldn't feel her toes.

"Colin, can you pick the lock?" Sadie asked.

"Love, I'm gonna pretend you didn't just ask me that," Colin said, and a moment later, the five of them were staring into the darkness of the mini mansion.

Sheets covered all the furniture, and the air was thick with dust. It wasn't Halloween, but it felt like a haunted house as they stepped into the shadowy space. The last time April had been there, she'd been trying to steal her key back from Evert and running for her life. Gabriel had almost died that night. Izzy had disappeared. And a little part of April hadn't survived at all — the part that thought her key was the most important thing in the world. The part that swore that April's mother loved her — that her mother would come back and make everything okay.

The dream April had had since she was two years old had died in this house; it had fallen over the cliffs and into the water and been swept out to sea, never to return again.

But now April was back, and there was a woman on the floor, bundled up in blankets, her lies turning blue on her lips.

"We've got to get her warmed up," Tim said. "Sadie, see if you can find some more blankets or maybe some of

Evert's old sweaters or something. April, go take a warm shower. Warm. Not hot. Sadie, can you find something dry for April to wear, too? Colin, you and Violet make sure all the doors are locked and start pulling shades. And nobody turn on any lights!" Tim warned. "This place has to look deserted. April? April!"

She heard Tim shouting, but she didn't really pay attention to the words.

"She's going into shock," somebody said.

"No," April told them. Hands reached for her, but she pushed them off as she fell onto a sheet-covered sofa with a dusty *plop*. "I'm fine."

"You're *not* fine." Tim took April's hands and rubbed them between his own, but she didn't feel the heat. She didn't want to feel anything because then she ran the risk of feeling everything, and who has time for that?

"April, look at me!" There was a warm palm on her cold cheek and brown eyes staring into her own. "I've got you," Tim said, and for a second, she believed he really did. "We're gonna get you warmed up, but first, did you hit your head? Are you hurt?"

April didn't feel any pain.

April didn't feel anything.

"Do we have any duct tape?" she asked instead. "Or we could use rope? We have rope, right?"

"Why do we need more rope?" Sadie sounded genuinely confused. "We've already got her inside."

"You think duct tape would be better?" April asked, considering. "Okay. Surely Evert's got some around here. I'll go—"

"April?"

"We have to tie her up!" April couldn't even believe she was having to explain it.

She really couldn't believe the look on Sadie's face, the tone of her voice as she said, "April, that's your mother." It was almost like she believed it. Surely Sadie wasn't that stupid? Sadie was the smartest person April knew! But Sadie was also the most innocent. After all, Sadie had had a mother once. She'd had a mother who was good and kind and loved her. All April ever had was a dream, and even that was disappointing in the end.

"April?" Now Tim was looking at her like she was crazy. They all were.

"You okay, love?" Colin asked, and April couldn't take it anymore.

"She is not my mother!" April pointed at the woman on the ground. "She was lying. Colin, tell them."

"Why are you looking at me?"

"Because you know when people are lying," April explained. "Tell them. Tell them she's just a madwoman with some swords. Tell them you know she was lying."

"April," Colin spoke so slowly that for a second April thought she must have zoned out and missed it. "I *don't* know that."

But April did. She knew it like she knew her own name. Except April *didn't* know her own name. She never had. And that was kind of the problem.

So she focused on the only thing that mattered.

"That's not my mother! We don't know who she is. We don't know what she wants or where she came from. We don't know—"

"April!" Violet never shouted. She rarely even raised her voice. So for a moment, April did nothing but stare. Everything was too raw. Too surreal. Even the sound of April's own heart was too loud, beating too hard in her chest. But when Violet spoke again, her voice was almost a whisper. "We know exactly where she came from."

Violet pointed, and April turned to see a painting

sitting on the floor, propped up against a wall like it was waiting for someone to come back and hang it in its rightful place. But its rightful place wasn't in the mini mansion. Its rightful place was in Winterborne House. Even in the dim light of Tim's flashlight and the bits of moonlight that filtered through the tall windows, April recognized the last portrait ever made of the Winterborne family. Gabriel's mother and father, brothers and sisters.

"What's that doing here?" Sadie asked.

"Evert stole all the Winterborne paintings from the museum, remember?" April said. "That one must have gotten left behind."

"There's no dust on it," Sadie said, just as Violet cleared her throat.

"As I was saying . . ." Violet went on, louder this time. Then she picked up the painting and placed it beside the woman who was lying on her back, eyes closed, like Sleeping Beauty. "She's not a madwoman. She's a Winterborne."

It wasn't possible. Violet was mistaken. But Violet had an artist's eye. She often saw things the others missed, so April looked between the woman on the floor and the family that had died in a terrible, fiery crash more than twenty years before.

Gabriel had been the only survivor. Everybody knew that. But as April leaned closer to the faces in the painting and the woman on the ground, she saw the resemblance to one of the girls in the picture. The same dark auburn hair. The same high cheekbones. The same beauty mark right beside her lip.

"She can't be . . ." Sadie started.

"Gabriel's sister?" Violet finished.

"It's not possible," Sadie said.

"Well, the evidence would suggest otherwise," Colin said.

"Maybe it's a coincidence." Sadie looked between the woman on the ground and the girl in the painting.

"If she is Gabriel's sister, it would explain why April had the key," Tim said.

"No." April shook her head. "It wouldn't."

"You always thought your mom was a maid or something," Tim reminded her. "But if your mom was a lost Winterborne, then that—"

"Uh . . . guys?" Sadie was kneeling on the ground,

pulling back the black shirt to examine the woman's wounds. There were cuts and scars, scrapes and blood. A massive bruise was growing along her jaw, and there looked to be a stab wound in her shoulder.

But then Sadie pulled back the rag that they had shoved there to stop the bleeding, and even in the faint light there was no mistaking the thin line that circled her graceful neck.

"What is that?" Colin asked.

"A tattoo," Sadie said. "Of this." Then she drew the shirt down just a little more, and they could see that the tattoo wasn't a line—it was a necklace. And etched into her skin in a place that April knew too well was the picture of a key.

Her key.

Her mother's key.

Her mother.

EIGHTEEN

THE SADIEMATIC ONE

I don't have a mother," April said one more time when Sadie found her in the long corridor on the top floor that ran along the back of the house, overlooking the cliffs and the horizon. She didn't care that her lungs weren't working right. She didn't even mind that there was something wrong with her eyes and they wouldn't stop watering.

Only one thing mattered to April, and it was that the world always understand . . .

"I don't. I don't have a mother. Never have."

"April . . ." Sadie crept closer. Like April used to do to Gabriel in the beginning. Like Sadie knew that, if she pushed too hard, April would open up those great big windows and jump, fly away like the ocean mist that always blew on the breeze. "It would explain why she had the key. If your mother was a Winterborne—"

"A woman gave birth to me, Sadie. And then she left me! I. Never. Had. A. Mother."

"Okay," Sadie said softly. "Yes. Of course. But if she really is that woman—"

"Then what, Sadie?" April should have felt bad for snapping. None of it was Sadie's fault. And Sadie just wanted to help—she always wanted to help, because Sadie was a good kid. April was the thing that was already broken on the inside—the thing that shattered in the mail but you don't know yet that it's in a million billion pieces.

April was Schrödinger's disappointment.

"What difference does it make, Sade? Is it gonna make the last ten years not happen? Huh? One time, when I was five, I spilled some milk, so my foster father made me drink it off the floor. To teach me to be more careful. Then I moved to a different house where my foster mother lost my shoes in a poker game. I wore her old slippers to school for three days before they called me into the office. I got in trouble. The principal said if I wasn't going to dress appropriately, the other children would find it distracting. They were more worried about what the other kids might think about the girl who didn't have shoes than they were about the girl, but whatever."

"April—"

"The nurse was nice, though. She said she found me some in the lost and found, but there was still paper in the toes. I didn't even know new shoes had paper in them. The next week, I got moved to a different home, and that one was nice, so . . ." April shrugged, but her eyes were all wet again. "Now you tell me, Sadie, if all this time I was a *Winterborne* . . . Tell me why I know that you're supposed to slip some food in your backpack every day during the last month of school so you have something to eat over the summer?"

"Oh, April . . ."

Sadie's eyes were wet then too. The mini mansion was entirely too dusty.

And then April was shaking again. Was it rage or shock, cold or fear? April couldn't tell anymore. She leaned against the wall and slid down to sit on her bottom. A buzzing sound filled her ears, like some kind of alarm was going off in her mind, telling her that something was terribly, terribly wrong. Or maybe that it was time to wake up. But right then it felt like the nightmare was never going to end.

She felt Sadie slide down to sit beside her, a warm presence at her side.

"Did I ever tell you about my first night in Winterborne House?" Sadie asked, and April shook her head and rubbed her eyes. "Mom and Dad were gone. And my grandma was sick. And this lady I'd never seen before had just shown up and told me I was going to her house, but it wasn't just a house. It was *Winterborne House.* Izzy showed me around and took me to our room, but then she just said good night and left me in there all alone. I'd never been so scared in my life."

April thought about her own first night—the dark shadows and creaking floorboards. It had felt like the house was full of ghosts, and she'd had Sadie and Violet for company. She couldn't imagine what it would have felt like by herself.

Sadie sighed. "That night I made my first invention. I thought I could sleep if I set a trap for anyone who might sneak into my room."

"Did it work?" April asked.

"Yes. And Izzy only needed three stitches, I'll have you know," Sadie said, and April laughed. "My point is, we all set traps. Sometimes they're made out of Slinkys and shoestrings, and sometimes they're harder to see, but we all do it when we're scared. When we're alone. But you're not alone, you know? Not anymore. Maybe that woman downstairs is a huge imposter. Or maybe she really is your mom and she's got a really good reason for doing what she did. We won't know until she wakes up. And then we can ask her. But, April?" Sadie made April look into her eyes. "No matter what she says your name is, it won't change who you are. Not to us."

Sadie shrugged as if she hadn't said much, but April thought that pep talk was the best thing that Sadie Marie Simmons had ever made.

It shouldn't have felt familiar. But it did. The five of them had lived together for months, getting bigger and stronger and closer, and yet it was just like those first weeks all over again.

The wind blowing outside, wet and freezing. The long-lost and presumed-dead Winterborne on the floor, sweating in spite of the chill.

"How is she?" Sadie asked as they crept back into the main room.

"Uh . . ." Tim looked afraid—almost guilty—as he

crouched over the still-unmoving body of the stranger. "Your mom—I mean, Gabriel's sis—I mean—"

"April and I have agreed that we don't know who she is yet and we're going to wait until we have more data," Sadie explained.

"Okay. But, well, we've got bigger problems right now," Tim said.

"Like what?" April said.

Tim tugged up the woman's shirt. "These are bullet wounds."

"Yup," Colin said. "That's a bigger problem, all right."

"Wait. I didn't hear any gunshots," Sadie said, confused.

"They're a day or two old." Tim pointed at the holes in her side. There was another on her shoulder. "Someone's stitched them up, but I'm pretty sure they're infected." He looked up. "She must have been in a lot of pain tonight."

"And she came after us anyway," Violet said, but April didn't care.

"Wait," Colin said. "If she was hurt the other night, then maybe it wasn't Gabriel who attacked Reggie. Maybe it was . . ." He trailed off but gestured to the woman on the floor.

"Why would she do that?" Sadie asked. "That doesn't make sense."

"Nothing makes sense," Tim said. "I think sense is something we're going to have to live without for a while."

"Why hasn't she woken up?" Sadie asked.

"She's just knocked out," Tim said, then shrugged. "I think?"

"Great. Another presumably dead Winterborne that we have to keep from becoming an *actually* dead Winterborne," Colin grumbled. "Want me to grab some supplies? I can sneak into the main house. I think we have something left over from the last time we did this."

"Our lives are strange," Violet said.

"You can say that again." Colin nodded, but he kept his gaze on Tim.

"Yeah. Bring whatever you can find, and . . . Colin . . ." Tim trailed off, then looked at April.

"Bring the duct tape," she finished softly.

At first it was like nobody heard it or understood, but a moment later Sadie was snapping, "No! April, you can't seriously want to tie her up?"

"We don't know who she is, Sade," April said. "Whether

she's my mom or Gabriel's sister or whatever . . . we don't know. But we do know that she broke in and ransacked Winterborne House and locked you and Violet in a closet. We know she hurt Gabriel and set the house on fire. We know she might have been the one who attacked Reggie Dupree—"

"That could have been Gabriel," Colin reminded her.

"The point is we don't know anything," April snapped. "And until we do, I'd rather not take any chances."

The wind picked that moment to blow harder, and April could have sworn it felt like ice.

She looked at Colin and said, "Be careful."

"April? Can I come in?"

Steam fogged the mirror, dancing in the glow of the candlelight. Even though the drapes were pulled and the blinds were closed, April felt safer in the darkness. She was at home there, all alone. But she wouldn't stay that way. Not if Sadie had anything to say about it. If it were up to Sadie, none of them would ever be alone ever again.

"I found some clothes," Sadie called through the door, and April said, "Come in."

Sadie looked sheepish as she stepped into the steamy

room. "They're gonna be way too big. But they're dry." She handed April a plain white T-shirt and a pullover from someplace called the Ocean Course, Kiawah Island, SC, but it might as well have read *International Association of Rich White Guys*. There were some sweats and a giant pair of old socks. "We can put your clothes in the laundry. They'll be done in a couple of hours."

"Thank you." April's hair was wet, but she wasn't shaking anymore. She was clean and warm as she pulled on Evert's too-big clothes.

"How are you?" Sadie asked.

"Fine," April said. Because she felt like she had to.

"The woman will wake up, April. And then we'll ask her what she knows about Gabriel and those guys who were after her — or you — or whoever tonight. She'll wake up!"

"Yeah. Is Colin back?" April asked, even though it was way too early for Colin to be back. He'd only been gone twenty minutes, and it was a long way to the main house, so April wasn't surprised when Sadie shook her head.

"No. But he'll be here soon. And we'll fix her up, and then everything will look better in the morning. You'll see."

Sadie was the smartest person April knew. If Sadie said

the woman would wake up, then she had to. Everything was going to be okay. April was going to be okay. If only that buzzing in her head would go away.

"What's that?" Sadie said.

"I didn't say anything," April said.

"No. That sound. What is it?"

It took April a moment to process what Sadie had said. "You can hear that?"

"Yeah. It sounds like . . ." But instead of finishing, Sadie turned and ran back downstairs. April was at her heels, and with every step, the sound got louder and louder until she could almost feel it vibrating in her bones.

When they finally reached the main floor, she shouted, "What's going on?"

She looked around and realized Tim and Violet were leaning over the woman on the ground, and for a moment April's heart leapt into her throat.

"Is she dead?" she blurted without thinking, without trying to understand how she felt or what it meant.

"No." Violet looked up. "It's her watch. See?"

And there, on the screen, were the words *perimeter breach*.

"I can't figure out how to turn it—" Tim started, but

Sadie pushed a button, and suddenly the buzzing stopped. "Off."

But the words were still there. Flashing. And the alarm was still sounding, but softer now. It was coming from Evert's study.

"Perimeter breach. Perimeter breach," an automated voice boomed as soon as April pushed open the door.

"What perimeter?" Sadie asked as, all around them, lights flickered on.

But not lights, April realized a split second later. *Screens.* It was like watching a brain come to life, neurons firing, synapses charging. Everything waking up, glowing in the darkness, showing . . .

"Winterborne House." April recognized the steps and the cliffs, the long hallways and huge sweeping rooms. Every monitor showed a different angle until they flashed again and April saw movement. There was movement in Winterborne House.

"Oh, it's just Colin." Sadie gave a sigh of relief.

And, sure enough, there he was on the screen, shoving food and supplies into an old pillowcase.

"I thought Gabriel tore out all the security cameras?" Violet asked.

"He did," Tim and Sadie said in unison.

Then, in the monitors' flickering light, April started to make out details of the room. It was like the command center they'd tried to make in Gabriel's cellar. But bigger. Better. More professional. Full of computers and equipment. Blackout curtains already covered all the windows, so April flipped on the overhead light and slowly turned, taking in every detail of a room that wasn't just a study anymore.

The cozy couches were pushed back, and cheap folding tables lined the walls. Metal racks held hangers covered with clothes. There were some dead plants and a bowl full of soggy cereal.

"I don't remember this room looking like this," Sadie said.

"It didn't," Tim told her.

"So . . ." April remembered the painting leaning against the wall in the living room. "I guess we weren't the only ones who had the idea to hang out in the mini mansion. But why would she set up all this? And how did she get cameras into Winterborne House?" Tim gave her a look, and April conceded. "Okay. I guess if she *is* a

Winterborne, she might know a secret passage or two, but why—"

"April," Violet said. "She was watching out for you."

And April didn't know what to say about that.

"Would it be wrong to say I'm kind of excited right now?" Sadie asked, staring at the computers and equipment with a quiet reverence. "Because I'm kind of excited—"

"*Perimeter breach. Perimeter breach.*" The warning came again.

"Darn it. How do I shut this thing . . ." Sadie trailed off when, on the screen, Colin walked across the foyer, into the library.

But Colin was not alone.

NINETEEN

THE FUGITIVES

Tim, wait!" April yelled, but she didn't actually think it would work. She didn't expect him to stop and turn back to the monitors and actually watch as Colin crept through the house, a half-eaten apple in one hand and that pillowcase in the other, like a tiny cat burglar, totally oblivious to the figure that moved just on the other side of the wall.

"We have to warn him," Tim said.

"The main house is fifteen minutes away, even when you're not trying to sneak around. By the time you get there, it'll be too late."

But no one said too late for what.

"How many are there?" Tim asked, searching the screens.

"I don't know," Sadie said as they watched, helpless and terrified, while Colin headed toward the library doors.

Then stopped. And turned.

"Is that ringing?" Sadie asked, trying to turn the volume up.

Onscreen Colin walked toward the desk that Gabriel sometimes used. He looked down at the telephone, but the ringing had already stopped. In the next moment, the library doors swung open and Reggie Dupree yelled, "April? Are you here?"

But Colin was already diving under the desk.

And Violet was hanging up the phone that sat on the table. "We have a landline," she said simply.

"Good thinking, Vi," Sadie said, but April couldn't say anything, because, onscreen, Reggie was stomping around the library, shouting, "April?" while Colin cowered under the desk.

"What's Reggie doing there?" Tim asked.

"Well, the last time he saw April, she was diving into the freezing cold ocean, so it might have something to do with that?"

"Violet, was that sarcasm?" Sadie asked. "Awww. You're growing up so fast!"

"You're just four years older than me," Violet reminded her.

But April never took her gaze off the monitors and the man who was opening the patio doors and shouting out into the night.

"April! Colin! Sadie! Are you guys out here? Are you guys okay?" Then he growled in frustration and ran back through the library and out into the foyer and up the stairs, yelling all the way. "Hey, guys! It's Reggie! I came to check on you."

But in the library, Colin didn't move. Reggie was lost inside the labyrinth of the second floor — his shouts probably muffled by all that stone and wood — by the time Colin slowly crept out from underneath the desk, then through the big double doors and into the shadows of the rocks and the cliffs.

Not a soul breathed until he burst through the mini mansion's doors a little while later, saying, "You're not gonna believe what happened!"

"Reggie Dupree showed up at the main house, and you hid under the desk until it was safe to sneak out?" Violet guessed.

"Okay. Maybe you will believe it."

. . .

Eventually, they settled the woman in one of the bedrooms. Tim disinfected and bandaged her wounds, and Sadie and April dressed her in dry clothes.

No one said anything about the scars that covered her legs. No one mentioned how it looked like maybe she'd been in an explosion a long, long time ago. All they did was clean her skin and treat her wounds and then tuck her in between the soft covers, where she no longer looked like a madwoman with two swords and at least one terrible secret. She looked like a princess waiting for a handsome prince to kiss her and wake her up. But April knew he'd probably get a knife between his ribs for the trouble.

When Colin pulled out the duct tape, he gave April one last look. "Are you sure about this?"

But April didn't even have to think about the answer. "I'm sure."

"But, April . . ."

"She broke into Winterborne House and ransacked the place. She attacked Gabriel. She *stabbed* Gabriel! Gabriel might be bleeding out in a ditch somewhere right now, and . . ." But April trailed off because she absolutely refused to think about that. "She was following us tonight. She hurt those men."

"You mean those men who were trying to hurt us first?" Sadie asked. "Those men?"

"Okay, maybe she won't hurt us. Maybe. But she's not exactly known for sticking around, so, yeah. We're gonna tie her up."

"And then what?" Sadie asked.

"And then she's gonna help us find Gabriel."

Because finding Gabriel was the only thing that mattered.

"Was that necessary? Do you really think your mom would just . . . leave? Again?" Sadie asked once they were all settled into the room with the screens and the computers and the blackout curtains. It was the safest April had felt in ages.

"Sadie, look at this place. Does this look like the secret lair of someone who wants to be president of the PTA?" April said because she couldn't say the hard part—that of course the woman would leave April. Everyone left April. Because April had never, ever been worth keeping.

It was easier to throw her arms out and gesture at the

computers and the weapons and the hodgepodge of clothes on the racks on the wall. In addition to a number of black capes and leggings and tunics, there were three pastel sweaters and a pair of khaki pants, some nurse's scrubs, a jumpsuit with a patch for a gas company, a black leather jacket, three sets of workout wear, and an honest-to-goodness ball gown covered in burgundy sequins.

Oh, and there were wigs. So. Many. Wigs.

"That's a valid point," Sadie said. "Ooh! I've always wanted to try bangs!" She pulled on a black wig while Violet tried to adjust a red one that was too big and kept falling over her eyes.

April felt cleaner and warmer, but far too weary and too worried to be in the mood for make-believe, so she sat beside Tim, who was busy counting cash.

"I've got just over ten thousand," he said.

"Dollars?" Sadie sounded amazed.

"Yeah. Not counting all that." He pointed to the stacks of Euros and pesos and a bunch of bills that April didn't even recognize.

"You know, I think she's better at this fugitive-on-the-run business than Gabriel," Colin said helpfully. "She could give him some lessons, because these" — he tossed something on the floor in front of where he was sitting cross-legged—"are good. No. Not good. *Great*. Amazing. Too good, to be honest." He leveled Tim with a glare. "Scary good."

"What are they?" Violet asked.

"Passports. Six—no, seven—of them." He sorted through the stack. "We've got UK. US. Australia. European Union. South Africa. Japan. And Brazil. And there are drivers' licenses, too. Twice that many credit cards. I don't think most of them have ever been used, but they'd work. I'd bet my stellar reputation on it. There's even a library card! I mean that's a level of detail that just . . ." He made the universal signal for *mind blown*. Then he tucked it all together in a nice little stack. "Whoever she works for or with or whatever, they are legit, and . . ." He trailed off and looked around, suddenly unwilling to go on.

"And what?" Sadie asked.

"Scary. They're scary, Sade. I know a lot of people who are good at bad things, but this . . . this is different. This is beyond."

For maybe the first time since April had known him, Colin wasn't teasing or joking or trying to lighten the moment. Colin really was scared, which meant April should have been terrified. But April had a long history of not doing what she was supposed to do.

So she just asked, "What's . . ." Her throat was scratchy all of a sudden. She almost couldn't get the words out. "What's her name?"

"Seven passports, love. Seven names. And not a one of them is real. But, April, if there's one thing I'm sure of, it's that her last name is Winterborne. Or it was, once upon a time."

"I'm more worried about who she is now," Tim said, and he wasn't the only one.

When April saw the eighth passport, she asked, "What's that one?"

Colin picked it up carefully, like it might explode. And then he handed it to her, and she opened it slowly. "That's the one she had made for you."

April didn't know what time it was. She didn't even know what day it was. Outside, the wind blew hard and sleet pinged off the old leaded windows and the only light came from the hallway, slicing across the room that still smelled like rubbing alcohol and sweat.

"April?"

"It's late, Vi. Go to sleep."

April might not have known what time it was, but her whole body was too tired — somehow heavier than it had ever felt before.

"But I came to tell *you* to go to sleep."

April saw Violet's shadow creeping across the floor, moving closer, but for some reason she couldn't take her eyes from the woman.

"Do you think I look like her?"

April didn't know why her voice cracked. She didn't know why her eyes burned. She just knew that one moment she was looking at a face covered in cuts and scrapes and bruises, and the next she was saying, "I can't decide if I look like her. I've never wondered that before. About anyone. But now I can't stop thinking . . . if she is my . . . then shouldn't I look . . ."

"You do," Violet said. "A little. Here." April felt soft fingers on her nose and then her chin. "And here. I haven't really seen her eyes, but . . ."

"But what?"

"I bet they're sadder than yours."

It said a lot that there could be anyone with eyes sadder

than April's. But then April had to remind herself that she'd been lucky when it mattered. She might not have had a mother, but that didn't mean she didn't have a family.

"No!" On the bed, the woman screamed. Her body jerked, trying to break free of the bonds, and then, just as suddenly, she stopped and collapsed. She actually whimpered, and Violet didn't seem afraid as she went to her and pulled up the covers.

"It's okay. You're safe, Georgia."

"What did you call her?" April asked.

"Georgia. It's her name. It's on the old pictures."

April's mother's name was Georgia. Georgia Winterborne. Gabriel's sister.

"Where was she?" April wasn't even thinking about the ten years she'd spent in the system. She wasn't mad for herself. "Gabriel was ten, and he thought his whole family was gone. That was *twenty* years ago! Where was she? Why didn't she come back? How did she survive in the first place?"

Then for the first time, April really looked at Violet. "What if she doesn't wake up?"

But Violet just shrugged as if it were the easiest thing in

the world. "Of course she will. She's gonna be okay. You're not gonna lose your mom, April."

"I know." April forced a smile. She didn't say what she was thinking: that you can't lose what you've never really had.

"April!"

April didn't recognize the voice, but as she bolted upright, she remembered.

She wasn't in her bed in Winterborne House. Izzy wasn't going to come in and tell them to get ready for class. Smithers wasn't frying bacon in the kitchen. And Gabriel might never growl at her again.

So April stared up at the little slice of moonlight that shone between the gap in the heavy curtains and let her eyes adjust to the dark before she looked at the woman who was trying to toss and turn on the bed, saying, "I'm so sorry. I'm so sorry." Her hands were bound, and she looked smaller, frailer, sweat beading on her lip.

"I'm so sorry," she said again, voice breaking.

"For what?" April pushed upright on the sofa and studied the woman on the bed.

Her head turned. *"Missing."* And then it was like she

was another person when she said, "You don't get to miss twice, chickadee."

The laugh that came next was pure evil.

"Don't listen to her."

April jolted at the sound of the voice, too close, too low, and when she swung her feet to the floor —

"Ow!" the voice cried, and that's when she realized that (1) it belonged to Tim, and (2) he was on the floor beneath her, a tiny pillow beneath his head, an old quilt across his body.

"What are you doing down there? Go to bed."

He turned over so he could see her better. "I'm in bed."

"Go to a real bed."

He punched the tiny pillow, but it was still too flat, too small. "Not leaving you alone with her."

She didn't even bother to roll her eyes. "She's tied up. Besides, if she really is my . . . *you know* . . . and if she wanted to hurt me, she could have done it when I was two."

"Okay." He closed his eyes and tucked his arms beneath the quilt. "Then you're not leaving me alone with her. Thanks. I feel safer already. Now go to sleep."

But April was already there.

• • •

"April! Where are you?"

This time, when the shouting started, April knew the voice. And April didn't wait. She threw off the blanket someone must have draped across her in the middle of the night, then jumped off the couch (and over Tim) and ran through the still-dark room and down the stairs as fast as she could.

"Gabriel!" she shouted. "I knew you'd come . . ."

But when she reached the den, she trailed off and skidded to a stop in the doorway.

"Sadie!" Gabriel was shouting. "Can someone please explain to me why there are bats in the library? No! Stay out there! The last thing we need is one of you going rabid."

April remembered the bats. It was a week after Smithers left, and someone had left one of the patio doors open. The five of them had huddled in the foyer, listening to Gabriel scream and shout for hours. He'd broken two vases and knocked over a whole bookshelf devoted to Greek tragedies, but eventually, the bats had been driven back outside.

They'd heard the whole thing. But right then, April was seeing it, watching on the many monitors as he chased and jumped and swatted with a broom. It would have been hilarious if it hadn't been so incredibly sad.

"Gabriel?" Violet's voice boomed through the monitors. "A woman's on the phone for you!"

"A little busy here, Vi! Tell her it'll have to wait."

"But—"

"I'll call her later!" Gabriel yelled again on the screen.

But April just said, "He's not back." And she felt like a fool. She of all people should have known better. People don't just come back. Or, if they do, it's never quite that simple.

"Oooh! Sorry!" When Sadie saw April, she reached for the controls and turned the volume down. "I didn't mean to wake you, I just . . ."

"She's been recording us?"

"Yeah," Sadie said. "It should feel creepy, but . . ." She gave a shrug. "I miss him."

On the screen, Gabriel had given up on the broom and was reaching for a sword, and April sank into a chair next to Sadie's and watched.

"How far back do they go?"

"Since a week or two after Evert was arrested. Gabriel

had someone come in and close this place up, remember? The recordings start a few days after that."

"So she knew the mini mansion was empty," April said.

"Yeah. But that wasn't exactly a secret."

"Hey." Tim's voice was soft, and his hair was sticking up in about a million directions as he eased into the room. "Bat day, huh?"

"Yeah." Sadie gave a little chuckle, and April couldn't blame her. It felt like another life—another time.

"Hey, Sade," she started slowly, "if she's been recording, does it show that night?"

"Yeah." Sadie clicked between a series of files and finally pulled up the video of Gabriel, all dressed in black, leaving for the costume gala. A few minutes later, Colin, Tim, and April followed.

Sadie clicked Fast Forward, and, on the screen, Sadie and Violet went about their business, all alone, until, suddenly, the lights went out. The cameras stopped recording.

"That must be when she cut the electricity," Tim guessed.

April expected the feed to go away—for hours of nothing but static. But a moment later, the pictures flickered to life again. But different.

"Whoa!" Sadie's eyes got wide, and April had never heard her quite so excited. Which was also quite terrifying. *"She's got battery backups and night vision!"*

Winterborne House looked different in black-and-white—darker and scarier. A house made of nothing but shadow and secrets.

"There you and Violet go to the supply closet," Tim said as, onscreen, Sadie and Violet used the light from an iPad to make their way through the pitch-black library. They opened the door and went into the closet and then . . . bam. The door closed.

"There she is!" April said.

"How did she get in?" Tim asked, and Sadie rewound the tapes and looked at the other feeds until . . . "There," Tim said, and Sadie stopped it.

"Did we know there was a secret passage there?" Sadie asked, and April shook her head, no.

"Okay," Tim said. "So she cut the electricity and then snuck in to . . . what . . . lock Sadie and Violet in a closet?" He glanced at the painting they'd propped up against the wall. "Steal a painting? I don't get—"

"Wait," April said, looking between the monitors, confused. "I thought these were all synchronized?"

"They are!" Sadie sounded offended that April would doubt her.

"Then if our mystery woman is in the library . . ." April pointed at the screen. "Who's coming up the cliffs?"

"Is that the same guy in the kitchen?" Tim asked.

"And in our room?" Sadie asked, her voice as calm and even as April had ever heard it, but April felt the tension as, on the screen, one of the men stopped for a moment in front of one of Georgia's cameras.

"It's the guys from tonight," Tim said, because of course it was.

"What do they want?" Sadie cried.

"Her," April said as, on the screen, one of the men crept into the library and Georgia sprung into action. It was dark and the images were grainy, but there was no mistaking those whirling blades, as Georgia danced and fought, spun and parried. They knocked over bookcases and lunged over tables, and at the first opportunity, Georgia ran for the library doors, leading the man away from Sadie and Violet.

"So she didn't break in to rob us . . ." Sadie said.

"No. She broke in to lock you and Violet in the closet,"

Tim said, but after what they'd just witnessed, it had a whole new meaning.

The other men found her in the foyer. One of them leapt from the stairs, but she used his momentum against him and tossed him against the wall, and then she was off, running toward the kitchen. They chased her down the halls, and for a moment they were out of the cameras' view, but in the stillness April heard it: gunfire.

"That's where she got shot," Tim said.

A moment later, the men came running back down the hall, away from the woman and out into the night.

"Wait." Sadie sat upright. "Where are they going?"

On the screens, the intruders all just . . . disappeared. "What happened?" Sadie asked.

"We happened," April said. It felt so strange, watching herself climb the steps with Tim and Colin, seeing Colin head off to fix the generator and Tim start calling Violet's name. Onscreen, Winterborne House was nothing but chaos and disarray as the kids made their way through the mess.

They saw Georgia return. They heard Gabriel yell. They saw the fight that seemed even more bizarre in hindsight. And when the lights flickered on, they all still looked like they were totally in the dark.

Eventually, Gabriel yelled at them and they all went to bed, but, this time, April was able to watch as Gabriel sank to the floor with the dagger, staring at it like he expected it to disappear at any moment. A few minutes later, he stood and went to one of the library shelves, pulled down a book, and began leafing through the pages.

He must have gone to sew up his wounds then because he disappeared for a moment, but fifteen minutes later, he was back. He drew April's key from around his neck, opened the Sentinel's chamber, and went downstairs.

Ten minutes after that, he was pulling on the coat that April had made him for his birthday and striding through the patio doors.

As far as April could tell, he never even looked back.

"And that's it," Sadie said, freezing Gabriel's face on the screen. "That's the last time we see Gabriel."

"That's because he's dead."

TWENTY

GEORGIA

Georgia Winterborne had been a beautiful little girl, with auburn hair and those Winterborne eyes and a little beauty mark just above her lip. She'd been a lovely teen. She should have been an absolutely gorgeous woman, but the figure who stood before them was the color of paper, and her eyes were wild and red-rimmed. She moved like even breathing was painful. Bits of duct tape still dangled from her wrists, but that appeared to be the least of her problems as she leaned against the door, surveying her former domain.

"Yes," she said to their unasked questions. "I'm awake. Also, pro tip: zip ties are better than duct tape."

"Is that because of the tensile strength?" Sadie asked,

intrigued. "Because I've been wondering if environmental—"

"Sadie," Tim snapped, and jerked his head toward the woman who was staggering into the room. Weak. Wounded. But still deadly.

"Where are the other two? Dead?" she asked.

"No!" Sadie cried.

"They're asleep," Tim said.

But the woman just shrugged and said, "Stay in this room. The windows are blacked out in here, but if you do wander off, at least have enough sense not to—"

"Turn on any lights. We know," Tim said.

"I knew you were the smart one," the woman told him, but he didn't look pleased, and Sadie looked offended.

"We know who you are," Sadie said, like she had to prove herself to this stranger. "You're Georgia Winterborne, Gabriel's sister."

The woman gave a little laugh as if it wasn't funny at all. "I'm whoever I need to be."

"No," Sadie said. "You're Georgia."

"Georgia Winterborne died, or haven't you heard?"

"Then why do you have that painting?" Sadie challenged. "Then why are you here?"

But those were the wrong questions. For ten years, April had thought about this moment and the things she'd love to ask: Are you my mother? Where have you been? Why did you leave me? Didn't you want me? What did I do to make you go away?

Why are you back now?

But those were questions about April's past, and April had to think about her future, so instead, she said, "Where's Gabriel?"

"I don't know," the woman said. It was the first time April really felt like she was telling the truth. She started rummaging through Colin's pillowcase and ate half a granola bar in one bite. Then she grabbed a bottle of pills and swallowed two of them without a glass of water.

"You said he was dead," April snapped. "Why would you say that?"

"Because either he is . . . or he will be soon."

"Did you kill him?" April asked, and the woman sat perfectly still for a long time, like she was locked in her own head. Like she was lost in a dream.

"Georg—"

"The Winterbornes are gone. Everybody knows that. Their boat blew up twenty years ago, and there were no survivors." She went back to the pillowcase, and this time, her voice was faint. "It just took some longer to die than others, that's all."

"But . . . you stabbed Gabriel!" Sadie shouted.

"I *grazed* him," Georgia shot back. "Which was his own fault. Trust me, if I wanted him dead, we'd be having a very different conversation. Still, if he went looking for me, he'll be dead by now. Probably?" She shrugged. Yes, actually *shrugged*. As if this wasn't the most important discussion of April's life. "People who come looking for me usually die. Of course, usually that's because I kill them, but . . ."

She shrugged again. "I'm sorry." She didn't sound sorry. "Gabriel's gone. And he won't be coming back."

"You're a liar," April snapped.

"Of course I am. But that doesn't mean I'm wrong."

"Who are those men? What were they looking for in Winterborne House? What do they want with April?" Tim asked.

"They don't want April," Georgia snapped. "They want me. And April is a convenient way to get to me, so . . . That's just math."

How many times had April said those words? A million? A billion? Those words didn't belong in that woman's mouth. April wasn't like Georgia Winterborne, not the pretty, privileged girl who went away or the scarred, scary woman who came back. They didn't say the same things or have the same quirks. They didn't even look alike.

But Sadie was already mumbling, "Genetics are crazy."

And April . . . April's throat was burning and her eyes were watering and she couldn't listen to another word.

She didn't stay in the room.

She didn't ask any more questions.

She did the thing that she'd been doing since she was two years old: she took care of herself.

She ran.

April had never been a fan of sunrises, but there was something peaceful about watching the black sky turn gray and then violet. It was like watching the world wake up as the first bits of golden light stretched over the horizon. April wanted to be as fast as that light. She wanted to see how far it went. She wanted to run across the water until she reached the other side. But that wasn't possible. So she ran until she reached Winterborne House instead.

She ran until she got home.

Then she threw open the doors, but she didn't yell for Gabriel because Gabriel wasn't there. April was going to find him, though. She had to. She'd find him and then he'd come home and then it would be okay to hope again.

Her key felt almost hot in her hand as she pulled it from the chain around her neck and opened up the secret room. If the video was right, then the intruders hadn't ransacked *that* room. Gabriel had. Because Gabriel was looking for something, and April was looking for Gabriel.

That's just math, April thought.

And then she wanted to cry.

She watched the stairs descend, then took off into the darkness, trying to see what Gabriel had seen, trying to find what Gabriel had found. The room had lain hidden—waiting—for decades. Evert had called it his family's "treasure." But, to April, it wasn't the prize. Gabriel was.

So she stood on the bottom step for a long time, taking in all the little things. There were sparring dummies and old capes, rusty knives and shiny swords—maps and compasses—not a single one of which pointed in the direction of Gabriel Winterborne.

Then April got busy. She sorted and tossed and stacked and filed and tried not to think too hard because thinking can lead to feeling, and feeling can lead to crying, and crying is for people who aren't in something of a hurry.

April had to find the book—the one she'd seen Gabriel take off the shelf in the library. If the video was right, then after the fight, Gabriel had sent the kids to bed, looked at that book and come down here. Then he'd strapped on his swords and lucky coat, and walked out the doors.

So the book was the key. It had to be. Which meant April had to find it. But there was nothing but old cups of stale coffee and piles of ancient paraphernalia and a trashcan that no one had emptied in ages, filled to the brim with stacks and stacks of paper, rumpled and ripped, all covered with Gabriel's writing.

Dear Izzy . . .
My dearest Isabella . . .
Hi . . .
Hey, Iz . . .

There were dozens of drafts, ripped into hundreds of pieces.

Please come home.
The kids miss you.
~~I~~
~~They~~
We need you.
I'll leave if you want me to. I'll stay if you want me to. I'll do
*   whatever you want me to.*
Because I need you.
I've always needed you.
I will always need you.
Do you know where Smithers keeps the light bulbs?

Okay, so some were more romantic than others. And they were all in the trash. But, most of all, none of them said where Gabriel was.

April couldn't even find one stupid book! How was she supposed to find a man who'd lived on the run for a decade?

She couldn't. And she was silly to even try.

The spiral stairs seemed steeper on her way up. The library seemed quieter. The halls seemed wider. When she finally made it to her room, she changed her clothes and brushed her teeth and seriously considered climbing into her own bed, because there was no sense in going back to the mini mansion.

Her mother was there.

April wanted to laugh at the irony. She'd spent ten long years dreaming about the day her mother would come back for her, but now all April wanted was for her to run away again. Then maybe she'd stop telling April things she really didn't want to hear.

But as much as the grownups in her life had no problem leaving April, her friends were the opposite, and if she was gone any longer, Sadie would send out a search party, so April pulled on her softest socks and her warmest shoes and she started down the stairs.

She was almost to the foyer when a hand slammed over her mouth and she was jerked off her feet and pulled back. April squirmed and kicked and grabbed a candlestick off a table. She was just starting to swing when a voice whispered, "It's me."

"Tim?"

He loosened his grip, and April turned to see him bring a finger to his lips in the universal signal for *shut up a minute*.

Then he turned his arm so April could see Georgia's watch on his wrist, the words as clear as day: *perimeter breach*.

TWENTY-ONE

THE QUICK CON

W ho is it?" April whispered in Tim's ear, the word more breath than sound. "Is it the commandos?"

Maybe they were after April's mother?

And maybe April would let them have her?

But she could actually see Tim's pulse—a subtle tic in his neck that kept pace with his heartbeats. He must have run all the way from the mini mansion, and when he shook his head he swallowed hard.

"Worse."

They were on the second story. From there, they could flee into the labyrinth of Winterborne House's stairways and hallways, passages and dumbwaiters. They could disappear. That might have even been the good thing—the smart thing. And being good and smart had never felt more tempting to April. But there were already footsteps in the foyer, so Tim grabbed her hand and pulled her behind the heavy curtains that draped across the window at the top of the stairs.

"Wait here," he ordered.

"Tim!" she snapped instead, because she didn't know who was down there. It might have been Reggie Dupree or masked invaders. But it wasn't Gabriel. It wasn't, and that was all that mattered to April.

And then she heard a knock at the door.

Did masked invaders knock? She looked at Tim, who winced as the door swung open and Colin's voice exclaimed, "Good morning, Ms. Pitts! How lovely to see you this fine day."

"Tim!" April gasped. "We can't let her in."

"We can't keep her out!"

Which was a moot point, it seemed, because the woman was already scowling down at Colin as if "excessive morning exuberance" were something that she had to mark off with her tiny pencil.

"It's always a good morning at Winterborne House, Ms. Pitts. And, if I might say, it's even better now."

Don't wink. Don't wink. Don't wink, April chanted in her head.

Too late.

He totally winked.

Then said, "And you're looking especially lovely. Is this new?"

The woman looked down as if she couldn't quite remember what dress she was wearing. "It is, actually."

"Beautiful," Colin said. "Just beautiful. Don't you agree, April?" He glanced over the woman's shoulder at where Tim and April were standing on the stairs.

"Uh . . . yes?" April tried, and Colin rolled his eyes behind the woman's back because April would never be even a semi-decent grifter.

"I assume your guardian is in residence this morning?" the woman asked.

"Of course he is," Colin said. "But first, can we offer you tea?" (They'd recently found a box labeled **SMITH-ERS'S EMERGENCY EARL GREY.**) "Coffee?" (They'd ordered some because if Gabriel ever came home, he'd probably need it.)

"No. Just an audience with Mr. Winterborne. Please. He and I have a most urgent matter to discuss."

"Right away, love. Here. Let me see if I can get him."
Colin sounded calm, but he looked nervous as he turned around and pushed a button on the SadieSpeaker. "Uh . . . Mr. Winterborne?"

April didn't know what he was thinking. After all, Gabriel wasn't going to answer. And when Gabriel didn't answer, Ms. Pitts would want to know why. She might even search the house this time. She might refuse to leave until Gabriel came home.

And Gabriel was never coming home.

Gabriel was dead. Except he wasn't. He couldn't be. Not when—

"Sadie!" Gabriel's voice came booming out of the speaker—so loud and so clear. It was the most beautiful thing she'd ever heard. And then she heard the rest of it. "Can someone please explain to me why there are bats in the library?"

The voice stopped. No. The *recording* stopped. April glanced up at Tim who looked almost as relieved as she felt.

Colin pushed the button again and said, "Oh no! Do you need some help?"

"No!" the Gabriel of several weeks ago replied. "Stay out there! The last thing we need is one of you going rabid."

Colin gave the woman his most earnest grin. "Our well-being is the most important thing in the world to him." Then he pushed the button again and said, "That lovely woman from Social Services is here. Should I send her in?"

"I don't think that's—" the woman started, but the recording cut her off.

"No!" it yelled again. "A little busy here—" The recording cut out quickly, omitting Violet's name. "Tell her it'll have to wait."

"But—" Colin said, following the script.

"I'll call her later!" the recording yelled, and then there was nothing but the sound of shattering glass.

"Well, if you'd like to wait . . ." Colin began, but the woman started fumbling with the zipper of her giant handbag.

"Wait? I can't wait!" the woman snapped, then pulled something from her bag with a flourish. "I need someone to explain to me how *this* ended up at a crime scene last night."

April recognized the jacket. She knew that soft wool, the way the tag scratched at the back of your neck. But, most of all, April knew the crest that was sewn over the heart.

But this wasn't April's jacket.

It was the one she'd last seen beside a chain link fence the night before.

"Hey!" Colin exclaimed. "You found it! Awesome!"

"So you admit that this is your jacket?"

"Yeah." Colin slipped it on. "Took it off yesterday on our tour of the new park — have you been to the new park? It's gonna be swell."

"So you admit you were there? Yesterday?"

"Yes."

"Not last night?"

She knows, April thought. It was all she could do to keep her voice from breaking as she asked, "What do you mean?"

"There was an altercation. Last night. And an explosion!"

"Oh no!" Colin cried a little too loudly. "Was anyone hurt?"

"No." The woman might have seemed just a little disappointed. "That coat was found at the site, though, and I knew it had to belong to one of you."

"Yeah. We toured it yesterday," Colin said coolly.

"The Winterborne Foundation is one of the sponsors, you know."

There was a crash in the library, but none of them even winced.

"This is silly. You don't have to listen to us. Mr. Winterborne can clear up the whole thing. The library's right through there." Colin pointed at the doors. "To tell you the truth, he'd probably welcome the help. He'll be able to answer all your questions, I'm sure." But Colin stopped with his hand on the knob, as if he'd just remembered . . . "Have you ever had a rabies shot?"

Another, louder crash came from the library just as the woman snapped, "No!" It took her a moment to gather up her bag and her clipboard, her tiny pencil and her composure. "That won't be necessary. This is obviously an . . . inconvenient . . . time. Rest assured, I'll be back."

And April didn't doubt it one bit.

They followed her to the front door and watched her walk out into the clear morning light. It wasn't until she was in her car and heading down the drive that Colin yelled, "Sadie! Tell Violet she can stop breaking—"

But another crash rang out just as they opened the

library doors to see Violet standing on top of the big table in the center of the room, dishes at her feet, shattered shards of pottery on the hard floor all around her and a pair of too-big plastic safety goggles covering her eyes.

"Well?" Sadie looked up from her laptop.

"She's gone," Tim said, and Sadie exhaled and sank down lower in her chair.

"Not to brag, but that wasn't a bad con for five minutes' notice," Colin started. "Bought it hook, line, and—"

Crash.

"Oops. That one slipped," Violet said.

Tim grabbed her under her arms, then pulled her off the table and put her down far away from the debris.

"You heard her." April crossed her arms over her chest. "She'll be back. She'll want to talk to Gabriel."

"Izzy might be back by then." Sadie sounded hopeful. "Or Smithers."

No one said that Gabriel might be back. And no one asked why.

The sun was high and bright, and the sky was clear by the time they made it back to the mini mansion, but April had to stifle a yawn. All she wanted to do was go to sleep and wake up when the nightmare was over.

But what April needed was answers. So they pushed through the doors and into the living room and down the hall to the den. They searched the bedrooms. Then the bathrooms.

But no one called out Georgia's name.

No one said a word.

Because April's mother was nowhere to be found.

Again.

TWENTY-TWO

April looked weird with black hair. She looked even weirder as a blonde. But eventually, she couldn't help it: she pulled on the long auburn wig and took a pen and made a little dot on the glass, at the very place on her reflection where the beauty mark had been on Georgia.

On her mother.

And then she stared at the girl in the mirror, hoping —almost praying—that someone else would stare back.

"Hey. There you are." Tim skidded to a stop in the hallway. "Sadie figured out that there are perimeter sensors around this house and the main house, so we should be . . . What's wrong?"

"Nothing." April tore off the wig and pushed past Tim and down the hall. When she reached the den, she threw the wigs on the table with the fake IDs and tried not to think about the irony. She'd spent ten years wondering who her mother was. Now she'd met her. Seen her. Talked to her. And she still didn't have a clue.

The woman formerly known as Georgia Winterborne was part ghost. Part enigma. But she was 100 percent gone.

"April?"

"Did you mean it?" she risked asking.

"What?"

"When you said you could take Violet—when you said you could run. Did you mean it? We have cash and credit cards. We can change the IDs, maybe? Could we just go away?"

"And look for Gabriel?"

"No," April snapped. Then she admitted, "Yes. I don't know. But perimeter sensors aren't going to keep the bad guys away forever. And eventually Social Services is going to wonder why Gabriel never shows his face. Eventually . . . Could we go . . . if we have to?"

"We could," he said, but it didn't make April feel any better. "But it's not going to bring Gabriel back."

"I know. You can save the speech. Gabriel hated us. Gabriel was never going to come back. Gabriel—"

"Was making a cake."

"What?"

Tim leaned against the table like he was suddenly too tired to stand upright.

"That last morning. Remember? He was making a cake."

"Yeah. So—"

"It was my birthday. At first, I thought it was a coincidence, but then we found Izzy's calendar. Remember? T'SBD? Tim's birthday. I think Gabriel might have been making a birthday cake. For me."

April remembered the mess in the oven and the smell of the smoke and the way Gabriel had been so excited— and then defeated. Because he'd been trying. He really had. And nothing had gone according to plan.

"Why didn't he say anything? Why didn't *you* say anything?"

"No one was really in a celebratory mood if you'll

remember, between the fire and the visit from Tiny-Pencil Lady."

"But, Tim, it was your birthday!"

"So? I don't care about birthdays. Not if you can't have one too." He couldn't face her after that, and April couldn't think of a single thing to say, so they both just sat in silence for a long time. Until April risked asking . . .

"So . . . what does that mean? About Gabriel?"

"It means I was wrong. It means I think maybe Gabriel didn't run away. Wherever Gabriel went . . . Wherever Gabriel is . . . I don't think he *won't* come back, April. I think he can't."

A cold front blew in that afternoon. Rain turned to sleet. A cold gray day morphed into a freezing black night. Even the stars seemed to go out, but the kids didn't dare start a fire, so they huddled in the den around a space heater someone had found in a bathroom, blankets over their shoulders. It was the kind of night that called for junk food and ghost stories, but there was only one scary tale on everybody's mind.

"Do you think she's gonna come back?" Violet asked with a shiver.

"No," April said. There wasn't any doubt. "If she wanted to hurt us, she could have done it."

"No. I mean, is she gonna come back so we can help her? Or she can help us? So we can help each other?"

"No." April shook her head. "I think she and Gabriel have that much in common."

They sat in the near-darkness, shivering in a way that had nothing to do with the cold.

"Do you think Gabriel knows? You know? That one of his siblings is alive?" Violet asked.

"And dressing up like the Sentinel and stabbing people because it's the Winterborne family business and all?" Colin filled in.

"That's funny," Sadie said, and everyone looked at her. "What? It is. All this time we've been trying to get Gabriel to be the Sentinel because it's his birthright or whatever, but some other Winterborne was already on the job."

"He was weird that night," Tim said. "Weirder than usual, I mean. Remember? After he fought her, it was like he'd seen a ghost."

"Because he *had* seen a ghost," Sadie said.

"But he didn't know it was his sister, right?" Colin said.

"I mean, she was wearing a mask. And she had that whole supposedly-died-twenty-years-ago thing going for her."

"No. Sadie's right," Tim said. "He was different after he fought her."

Sadie went to the computers and called up the video from after the fight. They watched Gabriel lean down and pick up the dagger. Even though the camera must have been far away. Even though the sound was faint. Even though they shouldn't have been able to see his eyes, they saw it — the moment when everything changed.

"There." Sadie pressed Pause. "He didn't recognize *her*."

"He recognized *the dagger*," April said.

"Yeah. Okay. So he recognized it." Colin shrugged like it was no big deal. "Makes sense. It's his sister's. Which means maybe his sister is alive. So he goes out to . . . find *his sister?* Where would he even look? The last place he saw her was the middle of the ocean."

"No." April couldn't take her eyes off the screen. "He'd go to the last place he saw *it*. We need the book."

"What book?" Violet asked.

April hit Play and, on the screen, Gabriel pulled the book off the shelf. *"That book."*

"What is it?" Sadie asked.

"I don't know," April said. "I couldn't find it in the lair, and believe me, I looked everywhere."

"Maybe we can zoom in and read the title?" Sadie tried, squinting at the screen. "We can get another copy and then—"

"You mean this book?" Violet asked, and April saw the old book in her small hands.

"Where did you get that?" April snapped.

Violet's shoulders jerked up and down. "The Sentinel chamber, where else? I like pictures."

Because that's what it was—pictures. Page after page of bright, smiling faces and those same blue-gray eyes. Year after year of Christmas stockings and birthday presents, Easter egg hunts and fireworks on the Fourth of July. It was what a happy family looked like, April assumed. Not that she knew firsthand or anything. It was what it meant to be a Winterborne. Except April was a Winterborne. Just a different kind.

"There." Violet pointed down at the picture of a little girl with a pointed hat and a cake covered with flaming candles.

"Whoa, whoa, whoa," Colin snapped. "There's a *private island,* and nobody ever told me? Private island, people! *Private! Island!* Do you have any idea of the cons you can run on a private island?"

But while Colin sounded outraged, April just felt sad as she stared down at the smiling family she would never know, standing in front of a big stone fireplace in a house that April had never seen.

"There! That's it," Violet said.

"I know. It's Georgia."

"No. There." Then Violet's tiny finger pointed to the place above the fireplace — at the sword and dagger that hung above the mantel.

"So . . ." Sadie said slowly. "Gabriel sees the dagger. Recognizes it. Then . . . what . . . goes out to the island to see if it's the same one?"

"Yeah," April said, feeling hopeful for the first time in a long time. "And if he did that, then *maybe he's still out there?*"

TWENTY-THREE

THE ISLAND

Found it!" For a moment, April was more than a little bit terrified of the look on Sadie's face when she emerged from the secret tunnel that ran from the mini mansion to Winterborne House itself. She was afraid there might be a SadieMatic waiting to catapult them to the island, but Sadie only pulled out a dusty map that led to a very different kind of treasure.

"There." Sadie pointed to a spot on the map. "I *knew* I'd seen it before! Smithers has a whole section of maps and things in the library. According to this, Winterborne Island is only ten miles away. We can do it. We can go get him."

April kept waiting for someone to argue or object or say, *Let's go tell a grownup,* but there were no grownups to tell. Not anymore.

"He might not be out there," Tim said, because someone had to.

"Or he might be," Sadie said, because someone
needed to.

"He might be hurt," Violet added, because that was the
thing that everyone was thinking. "He might need us."

But no one said the rest of it: that they needed him.

Half an hour later, Colin was running down the steps from
the house to the water and yelling, "All aboard!"

"What's all that?" April asked when she saw the giant
sack he had flung over his back like Santa.

"Provisions," he said, like it was the most obvious thing
in the world.

"It's less than ten miles," Sadie told him. "We won't be
gone all day."

"*If* things go according to plan," Colin countered.
"Which . . . When have things *ever* gone according to
plan?"

This seemed a perfectly valid question to April.

They climbed onboard the boat, and Colin started
going through his sack of goodies.

"We've got extra hats, extra gloves, dry clothes,

sandwiches, hot chocolate, water, energy bars, emergency flares, glow sticks, flashlights—"

"Colin, is that a pool noodle?"

"What? They float."

"You're literally wearing a life jacket. Right now. We all are," Sadie pointed out.

"Yeah. Well. Best not to take any chances," Colin said nervously. When Tim started the boat and eased it out of the little cove, Colin looked like he was going to throw up.

"Colin, are you afraid of the water?" April whispered.

"Water? No. Of course not. Being lost in a terrible storm and then freezing to death before you have a chance to drown? *Everyone* should be afraid of that."

And from that point on, April was.

So she sat with Violet on one side and Colin on the other as Tim drove and Sadie navigated. They huddled beneath a waterproof blanket, bracing against the cold spray that sprang up from the waves and the light drizzle that filled the air.

Eventually, land disappeared and there was nothing around them but gray sea and grayer sky, and April wasn't sure where one stopped and the other began. She wasn't sure which way north was. Which way *land* was. How was she supposed to find Gabriel if she couldn't even find Winterborne House? She'd only just found a home. It seemed a shame to lose it already.

"We should be getting close," Sadie said, but the wind was so strong that April barely heard her.

Tim slowed the boat down, and they drifted for a moment, bobbing on the water in a way that made April feel like she was going to throw up. Colin turned the color of old peas. Only Sadie sounded happy, because Sadie liked a challenge.

"We should be there! It's got to be close!"

"Maybe the map's out of date?" Tim asked.

"It's from 1980. It's not like it says the world is flat or anything."

"Can the compass be off?" Tim asked.

"We're lost." Colin gripped his Santa sack a little tighter. "I knew I should have brought more food. And water. And—"

"I'm using two compasses and a GPS!" Sadie snapped at Tim. "The chances of them all being off are minuscule. The island is around here somewhere." She squinted as if that could make her see through the thick layer of fog.

"What if you're not using them right?" Tim countered,

and Sadie leveled him with a glare that could have set the water on fire. "What if it's user—"

"It's not user error!"

"We're all gonna die," Colin whimpered, and April couldn't exactly blame him.

The tiny boat kept rocking and bobbing, and April felt as sick as Colin looked. What if Sadie really was reading the map wrong? Or the GPS? What if the island was lost to sea change or hurricanes or . . . something? What would they do then? If the island wasn't out here, then Gabriel couldn't be out here, and Gabriel absolutely had to be out here!

"Well, if the map is right and the equipment is right, then either the island disappeared or—"

"There!" Violet probably shouldn't have stood on the seat, but April was so grateful to follow her little finger to the place where something poked out of the fog. "Is that a tree?"

"*It's an island!*" Sadie sounded vindicated, but April just felt . . . scared.

She must not have been the only one, because Tim seemed extra special careful as he steered the little boat toward the rocky shore. The closer they got, the more they could make out. Tall pine trees and huge boulders. A steep hill and rocky cliffs. "Is that a dock?" Tim asked, and April leaned closer to the bow and tried to get a better look at the rickety thing that extended from the shoreline and out into the water.

"I think it was. Once upon a time."

"What is it now?" Colin asked.

"A death trap," April said. "But it's the best we're going to do."

Where are you, Gabriel? April thought for what must have been the thousandth time as Tim maneuvered closer.

"Let's find him!" Sadie exclaimed a few minutes later. "Let's — Ooh!" she yelled when her foot fell through one of the boards

"Look out!" Colin cried.

"Are you okay?" Tim asked.

"Yeah." Sadie was wearing heavy rain boots. "I'm not hurt," she said, carefully pulling the boot free. "But we'd better be careful. Half these boards are rotten."

So they tied the boat to multiple points using multiple ropes. (In hindsight it was possible they didn't need ten.)

But April didn't want to take any chances, and judging by the color of the sky and the way everyone kept looking up, she wasn't the only one.

They treaded lightly on the old boards as they walked toward the rocky shore that faded into a forest of dark, dense evergreens.

"It looks . . . haunted."

"You're not wrong, Vi," Colin told her. "Not wrong at all."

"Do you really think Gabriel's here? That he's been here the whole time?" Violet looked up at April.

"There's one way to find out." April reached for Violet's hand.

"Come on," Tim said. "Let's find the house from that picture."

The ground was wet and slick, and no one spoke again as they moved over the jagged rocks and toward the dense brush beyond the shoreline.

"Does that look like a path?" Sadie said, and maybe it did. The ground was slightly worn and the brush wasn't quite as thick, so that was the way Tim headed and they all followed—into the trees.

Everything seemed louder there—the sound of their boots on the rocks and the creaking of the trees as the wind blew harder all around them. It was darker than it should have been in the middle of the day, and April was glad when a beam of light sliced through the heavy shadows.

"Bet you're glad I'm prepared now, huh?" Colin said a little smugly as he held up his flashlight and stepped past Tim to push aside a leafy green limb. "Who looks like a genius—Ah!"

Colin screamed as something flew from the trees, swinging across the path. It all happened so fast. He stumbled back and fell into April, who fell into Sadie, and they all crashed to the hard, rocky ground while Tim grabbed Violet and shoved her behind him, screaming, "Is everyone okay?"

"Something's out there!" Colin said. "Something tried to get me."

Tim pushed Violet into Sadie's arms, then pulled out a dagger, and Sadie gasped.

"What?" he asked. "Colin's the only one who can bring provisions?"

Then he crept toward the tree. But he wasn't creeping nearly quickly enough for April, who jumped forward.

"For crying out—" She pushed aside the limb and came face-to-face with . . . someone? No.

"Aaah!" Colin screamed again when the creepy blank face came into view.

"It's a sparring dummy," April said.

"Like the ones in the Sentinel chamber? What's that doing way out here?" Sadie pushed forward as April stepped aside, revealing the sharp spike sticking out from what should have been the dummy's neck.

"Yup," Colin mumbled. "Very Winterborne-y. Very on brand. Not creepy at all." Then he climbed to his feet and tried to brush the mud and gravel from his backside. "Carry on!"

So April pushed aside the dummy and trudged on through the woods.

"Stay together. Stay close," Tim announced. "I've got a bad feeling about . . . everything."

And April couldn't blame him. There were bull's-eyes high in the trees. At one point they saw an arrow sticking out of the ground.

"What is this place?" Violet said.

"The photo album made it look like some kind of family getaway," Sadie said.

"Such a fun place to spend the summer," Colin said while he dug one of his emergency granola bars out of the emergency backpack he'd had in his emergency Santa sack back on the boat. "Fancy a game of volleyball? Want to toss around a Frisbee? Say, let's string up a dummy and shove a stake right through its—" But Colin didn't finish because he stumbled. And fell. The granola bar tumbled from his grasp, flying through the air until it landed. And bounced. And just . . . vanished. *Poof.*

"Uh . . . did that just . . . uh . . ."

"Disappear?" Violet filled in.

"Things don't disappear. That goes against science!" Sadie sounded angry, but that didn't stop her from being careful as she crept closer. "Unless . . ." Then she turned and looked around. Three heavy stones were stacked one atop another nearby, and she picked one up and flung it into the middle of the path.

April recoiled, expecting it to bounce. Expecting it to slide back down the hill. Expecting anything but the sight of that great big stone hitting the leaf-covered path and then dropping . . . like a stone.

Carefully, they crept toward the wide black hole in the middle of the path. As one, they looked over the edge and down and down and . . .

"Hey!" Colin exclaimed as Sadie dug through his backpack and grabbed a glow stick, cracked it, and dropped it over the edge. Light tumbled end over end before coming to a shattering stop twenty feet below.

"Yup," he said at last. "Very Winterborne-y."

But all April could do was look at that little light — the booby-trapped hill. And scream, "Gabriel!"

She wanted to run, but if the past two minutes had taught her anything, it was that running was very, very foolish. And April didn't want to be foolish. She wanted to be warm and dry and safe and back at Winterborne House with Smithers and Izzy and Gabriel. Even Growly Gabriel. Even the Gabriel who yelled at her and told her to get out of his cellar.

She wanted . . .

"Gabriel!" she yelled again, walking faster while, behind her, Tim shouted, "Watch your steps. Violet, stay with me."

"Gabriel!" April yelled louder, but the island didn't answer.

The path rose and curved, and soon April's heart began to pound as the house came into view. Except it was more like a cottage. Small and cozy. But broken. Like the Winterborne family itself.

April skidded to a stop, almost afraid of the porch and the door and whatever might lie inside.

The roof was half off. Some of the windows were broken. The stones were scarred and black, like a fire had tried—and failed—to wipe it from the earth, so it just kept standing there, abandoned and forgotten by the world. The door was ajar, and the wind blew it back with a deafening crack.

And then April couldn't be careful anymore. She took off, running, shouting, "Gabriel!" again, because he had to be there. He just had to. But as soon as she reached the threshold, she froze.

Because what she saw turned her blood to ice.

"April, is that . . ."

"Me," she said, not waiting for Sadie to finish. "Those are pictures of me."

Dozens of them covered one wall, and it was more than a little surreal to watch herself grow from a two-year-old with chubby cheeks and hair the color of a brand-new penny to a too-skinny kid with bloody elbows and holes in her shoes. To a girl in a plaid jumper with *Winterborne* over the heart.

April didn't know whether to be happy or freaked out that her mother hadn't walked away and forgotten about her—that her mother had been watching.

April felt the others moving around the house, searching all the rooms. But there was nothing but rotten food in the kitchen and towels on the floor. No blood. No notes. No clues.

"I suppose the good news is that *someone* has been here," Colin said from behind her, but April couldn't take her gaze off of the fireplace and the mantel where the sword and the dagger should have been. But it was empty. Of course it was empty.

"He's not here." April's voice sounded too faint and too small and far too far away. Like she was hearing it in a dream. "He might not have ever been here. We came all this way. We could have gotten hurt or drowned or . . . *He* could have gotten hurt or drowned. He's not here."

"April?"

"No." April shrugged off Sadie's hand. She didn't want anyone to touch her, because she felt dirty and stupid and raw. Everything hurt. Especially her pride. "He's not here." She didn't want to laugh. She just couldn't stop herself. "He's gone. He's probably halfway to Belize by now. Wherever that is. I don't know. Sadie, do you know where Belize is? I don't —"

"April."

"But, hey —" She didn't dare let Sadie finish. "We didn't make the trip for nothing. I mean now we know that someone has been stalking me, so that's super fun. And presumably that person is my mother. And presumably she, you know, took the time to booby-trap an entire island because that's what good mothers do, right? I wouldn't know." She threw her arms out. "Let's go. Let's get home before we run out of emergency gummy bears or what —"

"April!"

She spun on Colin, who was holding one finger in the air. "Listen."

Outside, the clouds were growing heavier and the sky was growing darker and there was a faint rumble of thunder in the distance.

"Yeah. We should hurry. I don't like the look of those clouds —"

"No," Colin snapped. But Colin *never* snapped. "Listen!"

And then April heard it. The wind was whipping through the half-ruined house and whistling through the trees. But no. It was an *actual* whistle, April was sure of it.

In the eerie yellow glow of Colin's flashlight, April saw Sadie's eyes go wide as the whistle blew three short blasts followed by one long one.

"The SadieSignal," Colin said.

And April shot for the door.

"Gabriel!"

It wasn't safe to split up.

It wasn't safe to move quickly.

It wasn't safe to be out there, on a nearly deserted and totally booby-trapped island, most recently inhabited by someone April was starting to think might have been a crazy person. Or a criminal mastermind. Or both. She was probably both. And April was really starting to miss the days when she wasn't anybody's daughter at all.

A fine mist filled the air, and the ground was slick and

damp, so April kept an eye on where she was going, but that didn't stop her from yelling, "Gabriel!"

Her throat was raw, and her voice wasn't as strong as it should have been. She felt the words fly away on the wind, but were they flying to Gabriel or away from him? There was no way to know.

So she stopped and listened for the whistle to come again.

"If Gabriel's stuck out here? If he doesn't have cover . . ." Sadie didn't have to finish.

The whistle sounded, and Tim shouted, "This way!"

They were walking slowly. They were being careful. But they were off the path, moving over rough ground covered by rocks and logs and bushes with tiny thorns, and it seemed like—booby traps or not—Winterborne Island was trying to kill them.

The thunder got closer and the black clouds flashed with lightning as the fine mist turned into a heavy rain, and April knew it was bound to get way, way worse before it got better.

Soon, water was gushing down the hill. The ground was slick and rough, and they couldn't even hear the whistle anymore. Maybe they'd never heard it at all. Everything was lost to the sound of the storm. Water poured down her face and into her eyes, and April couldn't see. She couldn't hear. She couldn't do anything but yell, "Gabriel!"

"We have to go back!" Tim shouted.

"No!"

"We can wait it out at the house! It's not safe out here."

"Gabriel's out here!" Gabriel had been out there for days. "Go back if you want to, but I'm gonna keep looking!"

And then April stormed off. Except she stormed a little too quickly, and the ground was a little too unstable and, suddenly, her exit was entirely too dramatic for her own good because April was lost in an avalanche of mud and rocks and water.

It was just like the park and the gravel all over again, because April's feet swept out from under her with a terrifying *swoosh,* and then she was on the ground and sliding down the hill, faster and faster. She clawed against the muddy ground until her hands burned and her fingernails tore, but she didn't even slow down a tiny bit.

"April!" someone shouted just as Sadie's second favorite rope unfurled at April's side.

She didn't hesitate for one minute; she grabbed it. Instantly, everything jerked. Somewhere, Colin screamed, but April stopped sliding. She lay for a long time, covered in mud and bruised by the rocks and suddenly happy for the hard rain that washed the dirt and debris from her tearstained face.

"April, are you—"

"I'm fine," she said when Tim finally reached her. "Thanks for that."

She should have turned over and crawled to her feet, but something kept her on the ground.

"Are you hurt?"

"No. I'm . . ." April trailed off when she saw them: three rocks stacked on top of one another like a little marker. Like a warning.

She wasn't sure why she did it. She didn't even know she *was* doing it until she grabbed a glow stick out of Tim's hand and tossed it into the torrent of water that rushed down the hill. She didn't even breathe as she watched the stick just . . . disappear.

"April?" Tim said, but April barely heard him. She was too busy scrambling over the rocky ground, desperate as she reached the edge of another pit just in time to see the glow stick tumble end over end and then land right beside the filthy face of Gabriel Winterborne.

"It's about time you got here," he growled.

And then he passed out cold.

TWENTY-FOUR

THE GIRL WITH THE KEY

G abriel? Gabriel, we're home."

He'd been awake when they finally got him out of the hole. He'd mumbled and grumbled and growled as they made sure nothing was broken and walked him to the boat. He hadn't even argued when Tim took over the controls and Sadie cast off the lines. Then, sometime between his second bottle of water and his third granola bar, he'd curled up and fallen asleep, and April watched him the whole time, counting every foggy breath.

Once they were back in the shelter of the boathouse, she leaned close and said, "Gabriel?" But she didn't touch him, because she didn't want to end up tossed through the air again—not without a pile of laundry to land on. She watched him stir to life, a water bottle still gripped in his hand, their thickest blanket around his shoulders.

"He's probably in shock," Sadie said. "I think he's in shock. Tim, do you think—"

"I'm not in shock," Gabriel snapped, but he stumbled when he tried to stand. "I'm hungry."

He did seem a little stronger as he turned and lifted Violet down out of the boat. He kept her hand in his as they started up the steep and winding steps, but the slicker the steps got, the steadier he seemed, and April watched him, knowing he was back but feeling like a part of him was still out there, lost and alone and a long way from home.

"He'll be fine."

April turned to look at Tim, who jolted when Violet slipped on the slick steps, but Gabriel caught her.

"You don't know that," April said.

"Of course we do," Colin said. "He's Gabriel Winterborne."

"Sadie?" April asked.

But Sadie only shrugged. "Does it matter what I think? He's not gonna go to the hospital either way."

April wanted to tell her she was wrong, but, as usual,

Sadie was 100 percent right, so she pulled up her hood and climbed the stairs.

Inside, she found Gabriel in the kitchen, trying to put water on for tea, but the stove kept making that *click click click* sound and the fire never caught.

"This blasted . . ." he grumbled to himself. "Smithers should have—"

"Here," Colin said, sliding Gabriel's hand off the knob before the whole house could fill with gas. "Let me. I'll make some soup."

"We don't have any . . ." Gabriel started, but trailed off when he threw open the pantry door and saw the fully stocked shelves. "Oh."

He seemed almost disappointed. Like he'd been cold and alone and afraid on that island and had envisioned the kids being the same. He looked like a man who couldn't decide whether he was happy or sad that they hadn't starved to death without him—like maybe the idea of someone needing him was something he'd just started getting used to.

"Gabriel, sit down," April said. "Please."

It must have been the please that did it, because he sank wordlessly into Smithers's old chair at the kitchen table.

No one sat in Izzy's.

"You'll feel better after a hot meal," Colin said, slipping into his favorite apron (**KEEP CALM AND CURRY ON**) and turning on the stove. "Hot shower. Good night's sleep. You'll be your old, grumpy self again tomorrow. As opposed to *this* grumpy self," he clarified.

"Thank you, Colin," Sadie said, but the words were a warning.

"Right-o."

For a long time, they all just sat there, listening to the hiss of the stove and the boom of the thunder and the sound of all the things that no one dared to say.

"I suppose you want an explanation," Gabriel said when the silence was finally too much.

"You recognized the dagger from the house on the island and you went out to investigate and fell in a hole because the island was booby-trapped," Sadie said, like it was the most obvious thing in the world, but from the look on Gabriel's face, it hadn't been.

"Yes. I suppose that sums it up," Gabriel said as Colin slid a bowl of soup in front of him. It was like he was summoning his strength. Or maybe just his courage. "I tried to climb, but . . ."

He looked down at his hands. They were shaking from cold or shock or maybe just rage. They were also filthy, covered in mud and blood, his fingernails all but gone.

"Gabriel!" Sadie gasped.

She got up and started filling a bowl with hot water.

"I couldn't climb out." He laughed, but it wasn't funny. "I should have been able to . . . but the sides were steep, and when I fell, I dislocated my shoulder." Tim started to move toward him, but Gabriel waved him off. "I got it back into its socket, but I wasn't strong enough. I told myself that in a day or so I'd be able to make the climb, and as long as it rained occasionally I could live for a while. But the rain kept the sides slick so . . ." He shrugged. "And then . . ."

"What?" April had to know.

"I told myself the five of you would find me." He laughed again. Then something seemed to occur to him. "How *did* you find me?"

"We recognized the knife from the picture," April said. "Are you sure you're okay?"

"Yes. I am. Really." He looked her right in the eye — a look that said, *Pay attention. This is important. I really mean it.* "I lived rough for ten years, April. I can handle a few days in a hole." He took a sip of his soup then. Slowly. Carefully.

As if he didn't quite trust Colin's cooking. Then he looked at the empty chair and asked, "Any word from . . . anyone?"

Where were they even supposed to start? With the masked intruder-slash-mother or the gunmen at the park or the Tiny-Pencil Lady who never seemed to leave them entirely alone? But Gabriel wasn't asking about them. Not even about Smithers.

So April just said, "She'll come back. If she knew you were hurt—"

"No," he snapped.

"But she'd want to—"

"No one can know," he said in a way that told April he wasn't just talking about his pride. He finished his soup, pushed the bowl away, and told the group, "I need to speak with April for a moment. Alone."

He wasn't asking. It wasn't a question. But absolutely no one moved.

"Now," Gabriel growled, and April couldn't help herself. She leaned close.

And whispered, "Is this you trying to break it to me that your sister didn't die in the shipwreck and also she's my mother and possibly a little bit insane and/or super scary?"

"She also might be a spy," Colin added helpfully. "That's my theory. Ooh. Or an *assassin*. Or *spysassin*."

This time it was Gabriel's turn to stare, slack jawed.

"We've been busy," Colin explained with a shrug. He got up and went to the stove. "You want another bowl of soup?"

But Gabriel just said, "Out. I won't ask again," and this time no one argued.

Only Sadie and Violet lingered a moment.

"Go on," he said. "Put on some dry clothes and—"

"I'm just so glad you're home!" Violet threw her arms around him while Sadie took the other side.

April had never seen Gabriel look less comfortable than when he was surrounded by crying girls.

"Please don't ever go away again!" Sadie wailed, and Violet cried, and Gabriel stood there awkwardly, not promising any such thing.

"I'm fine," he tried. "There. There." He patted their heads. "I'm okay. Now go. Warm up before you get sick."

When they finally pulled away and started for the door, April heard Sadie mumble, "That settles it. I'm making trackers for everyone. From now on . . . trackers in shoes and trackers in bags and trackers in belts and . . ."

The kitchen door swung shut, and April was all alone with Gabriel. It had been a long time since he'd been her own personal billionaire, and even though she'd never in a million years admit it, she'd missed that.

She'd missed him.

When the kettle started to scream, she got up and poured hot water over a bag of Smithers's Emergency Earl Grey, then brought the cup to Gabriel, who wrapped his hands around it like he still couldn't quite get warm.

"I'm sorry."

For a second, she was sure she'd misunderstood. She wondered if he'd even spoken at all. Or maybe he was speaking to the tea. Or to Smithers. Or to the ghost of Izzy that still haunted the whole house. But Gabriel kept talking, and that might have been the scariest part.

"That night, I shouldn't have yelled at you. I shouldn't have left without telling someone where I was going, but I thought I'd be back by morning. I'm sorry, April. You must have been terrified."

"We were a little scared," she told him. "But more than anything, we were . . . confused." It seemed as good a word as any.

He leaned back in his chair, as if to see her from a

different angle. She could practically see the gears working behind his eyes and then he tensed, realizing. "You
thought I left you."

April could do nothing but shrug. "Maybe. I wasn't
sure."

"But the others . . . they *were* sure?"

April gave another shrug. "At first, Tim and Colin . . .
they thought you . . . you know . . . left us. Sadie and Violet thought you were dead in a ditch somewhere." She
looked at him. "By the way, this is the part where you're
supposed to say, 'Oh no! You kids mean the world to me,
and I would never, ever abandon you,'" she said in her most
growly — most Gabriel-y — voice.

And he looked like he wanted to laugh. Like he wanted
to smile but had forgotten how.

"I'm supposed to say that, am I?" he asked.

April gathered up his empty bowl and spoon. "Wouldn't
hurt." But before she could take them to the sink, she
stopped. "Gabriel, are you okay?"

She wasn't talking about dislocated shoulders or dehy-
dration or whatever nasty infection his stab wound must
have had by then. She was asking about something way,
way bigger than just life and death.

And he knew it because he didn't face her when he said, "No, April. I'm not."

"It'll be okay," April blurted, because that was what people were supposed to say. Especially when it wasn't true.

But when Gabriel said, "Will it?" it sounded like he was actually asking. "My sister is alive. She's been alive for twenty years and never told me. Even when she had you, she didn't tell me. She didn't ask for help."

"Yeah. Gee. I've never known anyone like that before," April said, but Gabriel didn't even scold her for her sarcasm. Then something else occurred to her. "So you didn't know? About me?"

He looked like she'd slapped him. "Of course I didn't know."

But he was a little too slow. A little too indignant. And April knew . . .

"Yes. You did."

"It's getting late, April. You should go to bed."

"How long? How long have you known that you're my . . . uncle." April's voice cracked. It was the first time she'd said the word. The first time she'd really even let herself think it.

Gabriel was her uncle.

But it didn't make her happy like it should have. It made her angry.

"How long have you—"

"Since the first time I saw your key!" he snapped, then realized he'd made a terrible, terrible mistake, because something inside of April was breaking and she was starting to regret not leaving him in that hole.

"You lied to me."

"I never lied." Gabriel shook his head.

"You knew who my mother was, and you—"

"My sister was dead, April! They were all *dead,* and they had been since I was ten. Of course I didn't think my dead sister was your mother."

"Then what *did* you think?"

Gabriel took a deep breath and slouched like maybe fighting with the niece you didn't know you had was harder than it should have been.

"I just knew something didn't make sense." Silver eyes found hers, and when he spoke again, it was almost like a prayer. "I knew you mattered, April."

And just like that, April felt her heart break. She'd never mattered before, and it shouldn't have hurt, but it did. Because April didn't matter because of her laugh or her smile or her wit or her courage. April mattered because, when she was two, someone put a key around her neck and walked away.

The girl with the key mattered to Gabriel Winterborne. But April? April was just the thorn in his side.

"I'm sorry. You must be so disappointed."

"Why would you say that?" he asked.

"Gabriel?"

April almost didn't hear the voice, but she saw the kitchen door open a crack and Sadie peek in, like she'd been waiting for the shouting to stop and thought maybe, at last, the coast might be a little bit clear.

She was wrong.

"Not now," he snapped.

Sadie winced, but she didn't back away.

"I know, but, see, there's —"

"I said *not now!*" he roared, but the kitchen door was swinging open and a woman was pushing in.

Clipboard poised.

Tiny pencil ready.

And a very small, very smug smile upon her face as she said, "*Mr.* Winterborne . . . it's past time I speak with you."

TWENTY-FIVE

WE ALL FALL DOWN

Gabriel didn't take their visitor to the library. Of course he didn't. Because the kids could totally spy on visitors in the library, and he obviously didn't want that, and April couldn't shake the feeling that she was being punished.

So she sat on the soft runner that lined the stairs, looking down on the foyer below. From there, they'd surely hear when the woman finished yelling at Gabriel. Except the yelling had never started. And that was the scariest thing of all.

"He's in so much trouble," Sadie was saying. She had her second favorite toolbox and was hard at work on what would no doubt become the next generation of SadieSonics. Some people stress eat. Some people stress pace. Sadie stress invented. And April knew better than to interfere.

"It's not that bad" Violet said. "I mean Gabriel's here now. And there's food and heat, and none of us are bleeding . . ."

"Gabriel might be bleeding," Colin reminded them.

"Well, no children are bleeding. No bleeding children has to be a good sign, right?" Violet asked, but Tim just looked at April over the top of Violet's head.

And the two of them said, "Sure?"

"Of course!" Sadie exclaimed. "She doesn't know what she doesn't know. She just knows that she doesn't know everything, which means she might not know *anything*." She made her ta-da hands, but it sounded like the person she most wanted to convince was herself.

"It might not be that bad, but it's not good either, Sade." Colin wrapped his arms around his knees. "Little Miss Tiny Pencil knows something's off around here. And you know she heard Gabriel yelling. She probably couldn't figure out what he was yelling *about,* but it wasn't the best first impression. Or second. Or . . . third."

"Gabriel's home," Violet reminded them. "That's all that matters."

And April knew she was right. She also couldn't shake the feeling that something was really, really wrong.

The rain had turned to sleet, and it pinged against the window, like something was outside, fighting to get in, and all April wanted to do was bar the doors.

"Children?" Gabriel's voice echoed in the big old house.

"We're here," Tim called, and then Gabriel stepped into the foyer and looked up at them, but his gaze stayed focused on April. Something about it made her want to run. And hide.

"Might I ask you to join me in the study?" It was the most Un-Gabriel-y thing she'd ever heard.

He was entirely too calm and quiet, and she must not have been the only one who thought so, because Colin whispered, "Did he have a head injury?"

"No," Tim said.

But Colin shrugged and pushed on. "Sure sounds like a head injury. I think he thinks he's Smithers."

But they got up anyway and went downstairs.

They found Tiny-Pencil Lady in a room with hard chairs and stuffy draperies and nine million things that looked completely and utterly breakable. Needless to say, April had never spent any time there. Ms. Pitts, however, looked quite at home as she moved around, perusing the shelves and picking up knickknacks and checking for dust.

"Hello, children. Come in," she said, like it was her room in her house and the kids were now her problem. "As you know, I have tried repeatedly to ascertain the situation here."

She moved around the room as she talked, eyeing the five of them, who stood in a straight line, almost at attention. As if they were little toy soldiers all in a row. Or dominoes; there wasn't a doubt in April's mind that with a single flick of her tiny pencil, that woman could make them all fall down.

"I had hoped that the changes here would be a minor inconvenience, but it has become clear that in the absence of a proper administrator, this *home*"—she actually made little finger quotes around the word, like it wasn't a home at all—"now poses an inhospitable living situation."

There was a small crystal globe on the mantelpiece, and the woman picked it up and turned it to catch the light, as if the earth—and all the people on it—were at her mercy. But April's entire world was in that room. And she already felt dizzy.

"I expect Mr. Smithers will be home soon," Gabriel

said. "If we seem disheveled, it's because the children and I have been on a field trip to Winterborne Island, doing . . ."

"Geological studies," Sadie filled in.

"I don't care," the woman said simply. "I suspected this might be the case, but I can see now I have no choice. These children are at risk and will be removed from this home, pending further review."

"No," Gabriel said.

"I'm sorry. Did you think this was a discussion?"

"The children are fine," Gabriel snapped. "We're fine. We have everything we need."

"You don't have my approval, and rest assured, sir, you need that."

"I'm sure we can come to some arrangement."

"Are you offering me a bribe?"

"Would that work?" Colin sounded hopeful until Tim stepped on his foot. "Ow!"

"Ms. Pitts," Gabriel said, "I will admit it's been a bit of an adjustment, but the children and I—"

"You were missing for . . . what was it? Ten years?" she asked calmly. "Your uncle is in prison for murder and arson and a whole host of nasty business. You've made one public appearance since your return, during which one of the children managed to fall off of a balcony in front of half the city."

"Yes," Colin added helpfully. "But he caught her!"

Ms. Pitts didn't care. April wasn't sure she'd even noticed.

"Do you honestly think these children can be happy here?" she asked.

"Yes!" Gabriel said, and the woman crept closer.

She was at least six inches shorter, but it felt like she was looking down on him when she said, "What about you, Mr. Winterborne? Are *you* happy here?" But Gabriel didn't say a single word. She started for the door, but not before handing the small globe off to Gabriel and pulling a walkie-talkie from her purse. "Yes. It's time. Let's get this done."

The sky flashed, and the woman was out into the foyer before the thunder had caught up with the lightning. April didn't know what she'd meant, and she wasn't the only one running along in her wake. But when the front doors flew open, she froze, because the foyer was filling with sheriff's deputies and the woman was saying, "Children, get your things. You have five minutes. These officers will help you —"

"No," April ordered. "We're not going anywhere."

"There has to be some kind of mistake!" Sadie blurted, looking for reason.

"No mistake," Tiny-Pencil Lady said. "Now, if you don't need to pack your things—"

"I don't need to pack because I'm not going anywhere! Gabriel?" April tried to get his attention. When he didn't turn, April yelled, "Gabriel!" Then he came back and pulled her into his arms and carried her toward the door.

She pounded on his shoulders, but he didn't even flinch. He just carried her to the little alcove—the one with the old coats and smelly umbrellas where she'd lain in wait for him about a million years before.

"Here," he said, dropping her and shoving a heavy coat and one of Izzy's hand-knitted hats in her direction. "You don't want to catch cold."

It was almost paternal. It was almost like he cared. But he didn't care. He couldn't have. April wasn't a sword, after all. She wasn't a twenty-year vendetta. She wasn't the thing he ran to. She was the thing he'd run from.

And now it was April's turn to go away.

"There!" She ripped off her key and slammed it into his hand. "That's all you wanted anyway."

But Gabriel didn't talk. Or yell. Or even growl. He just

slipped the key into his pocket, then looped one of Izzy's scarves around April's neck. His hands lingered there for just a moment. Like maybe hugging was something he ought to try but he didn't want to fail at.

"Don't do this," she whispered. Her voice broke. "Please. Please don't make me go. I'll be good. I won't make messes or talk back. I'll be good. I will be. I—"

"It's for the best."

"No." She couldn't even see him then. Her eyes were too fuzzy. "You're what's best for me," she said, then wiped her nose on Izzy's itchy scarf, and Gabriel closed his eyes real hard.

"I'm not what's best for anyone."

"Children!" Tiny-Pencil Lady called. "Children, it's time to say goodbye to your former guardian."

"Where are you taking us?" Sadie looked like April felt.

"You can't take us," Violet said, even though Violet almost never talked to strangers. "Gabriel, don't let them take us. Gabriel!"

Violet yelled and Colin kicked and Sadie cried, but April just looked at Gabriel, who clutched that little globe like he might be planning a trip now that there were no kids tying him down.

"Gabriel?" Tim asked, staring as if, at any moment, someone was going to break out the swords, but there was just a subtle shake of Gabriel Winterborne's head. As if he couldn't be bothered to do more.

"Officers," the woman said, "I believe the children need your help finding the door."

"No," Sadie said. "No. I live here. I live here! You're making a mistake. This is my home! This is my home!"

"We're not going anywhere with you," Colin said. "You can't make us!"

But then they made them.

April remembered very little from the moments that followed. She couldn't distinguish rain from tears or fear from anger.

All she heard was a deep, haunting scream and the sound of breaking glass.

But, to April, it was just the sound of her whole world shattering.

TWENTY-SIX

YOU DON'T GET TO PICK YOUR FAMILY

Colin still had his backpack.

Of all the thoughts that ran around in April's head, that was the one April came back to time after time.

As they drove away in a van.

As they settled into a big, new house with instructions that they were to be placed with new families in the morning.

As the girls were locked in one room and the boys taken to another.

April had gone through this routine a dozen times in her life, but this time felt different. Because this time Colin still had his backpack.

"I miss Gabriel." Violet nestled into Sadie, and Sadie looked straight ahead, her eyes a little glassy. Like she was sleepwalking. Like this was a nightmare and she was going to wake up at any moment, back in her own bed.

"April?" Violet looked up at her. "When will Gabriel come for us?"

Never, April thought but didn't say. Gabriel had lied about April's key, so April wanted to hate him. And maybe she would have. If she hadn't missed him so very, very much.

"April?" Violet tried again.

So April admitted, "I don't know."

"Izzy will come home now." Sadie sat up straighter, and her eyes seemed to focus. It was like her brain was a computer that had finally shot out the correct answer. "That's it. This will do it. Izzy will come home, and we'll go back to Winterborne—"

They all jumped when there was a pounding on the window.

"It's your mom!" Sadie said, looking at the glass.

"It's Gabriel!" Violet guessed.

The knock came harder, rattling the glass, but April knew it wasn't the wind. Even then, she wasn't quite ready for the sound of Colin saying, "Open the bloody window! It's freezing out here!"

"Are you crazy?" she asked as she helped pull him in. He was sopping wet and shivering, and Tim didn't look any better as he tumbled onto the cheap, thick carpet.

Sleet blew through the window, little needles pricking April's skin, so she slammed the window shut behind them.

"What are you doing?" Sadie cried. She looked out the window. "Are you insane? That ledge can't be more than fifteen centimeters thick!" (Because when Sadie was upset, she was usually upset on the metric system.)

"We're here to rescue you," Colin said.

"You were the ones who needed rescuing!" Sadie countered.

"Easy, Sade." Colin took one of the towels that Violet had brought them. He seemed calm. Almost optimistic. "It's barely a climb at all. And, besides, it was worth it."

"Worth it how?" Sadie asked.

"Because of this." Then Colin tipped his backpack onto the bed, spilling out bottles of water and food and extra glow sticks and Band-Aids. Her mother's watch. And passports. And credit cards. And cash — so much cash. It wasn't everything from April's mom's supplies at the mini mansion, but it was enough.

And it didn't take long for Sadie to put it all together. "You want to run away?" April could tell by the look on her face that it was the first time she'd ever done math and not liked the answer.

"We don't *want* to," Tim snapped. "But if we stay, we get split up. You might not know how the system works, but the rest of us —"

"Izzy's going to come back!"

"You don't know that, Sade," Colin countered.

"She will. She has to."

"And what then?" Colin snapped. "You think Tiny-Pencil Lady's going to say, 'Oh, the woman who abandoned the kids to the madman's care is back. Yes. Right. Let's ship them back now, shall we?' No. We had a good run. But it's over."

"We had a good run, so now we have to run. Is that it?" Sadie asked.

"Gabriel's going to come for us," Violet said.

"Gabriel could have fought for us an hour ago, but he practically pushed us out the door," April said. She picked up the watch and fingered it nervously, but she didn't feel any closer to her mother. Or her uncle. "He didn't even . . ." Her voice cracked. "He didn't even say goodbye."

"Look." Colin's voice was low and even. "We've got money. *Resources*. We've been basically on our own for days. And, besides"—he looked sheepish—"we wouldn't be alone. We'd be together."

"Where would we go?" Sadie asked, considering it. "The mini mansion?"

Colin and Tim shared a look, then Tim said, "Maybe," in a way that really meant *no*.

"We can do it, Sade," Colin said.

"No. Smithers will be back soon. And Izzy. And then—"

"Fine." Tim shot to his feet. "Stay. Violet?" He reached down for the little girl, but for the first time, Violet didn't reach back.

"I want Gabriel." She nestled into Sadie, and Tim dropped to speak on her level.

"I don't think we're gonna get to live with Gabriel anymore, Vi. But we can stay together. I promise."

People made promises all the time. Every day. They promised to love and cherish. They promised to come back for two-year-old babies and mysterious keys. Promises weren't made to be broken, but hearts were. And April couldn't shake the feeling that hers wasn't going to heal anytime soon.

"*What* is going on here?" Ms. Pitts didn't have her tiny pencil. Or her clipboard. But she looked like maybe she'd just been hit with a pancake and an egg and maybe the contents of an entire refrigerator all at once, because she was standing in the doorway, hands on her hips and fire in her eyes.

"You two!" She pointed at Colin and Tim. "How did you get in here?" Then she noticed the damp windowsill, and her voice went up an octave. "Did you climb . . . Were you out . . . How dare you—"

"Well, it's like this, love," Colin started. "The girls get scared sometimes without us around for protect— ouch . . ." Colin looked down at Sadie who gave a quick shake of her head.

"I will deal with you later!" Ms. Pitts pointed at Colin. "But first I need a word with April."

"Hey, I didn't climb out any windows." (Yet.)

"Downstairs." Ms. Pitts stepped aside and waited for April to pass, but April didn't move. "Now!"

Someone had had the presence of mind to throw a

pillow over Colin's pile of loot, but April glanced at it on her way to the door. She glanced at all of them, as if expecting to see them disappear like smoke.

As if she'd never had friends at all.

The house smelled funny. Stale and dusty, like it had windows that hadn't been opened in a long time and trashcans someone forgot to clean before they left. But maybe April was just used to Winterborne House. It was also dusty and had rooms that saw entirely too little sunlight, but sometimes it smelled like lemon polish and soup that had been simmering all day and antiseptic from whatever wound they'd had to dress. April missed it. She missed it so, so much. And she knew there was no medicine for the parts of her that hurt right then.

When the woman reached the first floor, she said, "April, I have some wonderful news. How does that sound?"

But April merely huffed and said, "Unlikely."

Ms. Pitts scowled down like she knew she was supposed to laugh but laughing was beneath her.

"Do you have your things?"

On instinct, April's hand went to her neck because her

key had always been her prize possession. But it wasn't *her* possession. It was her mother's. It was Gabriel's. And it was gone now, so April had to say, "I don't have any things."

"Very well. Then come with me."

That's when April realized what the women was really saying. "No!" She dug her heels in. "You said we'd be placed in the morning. You can't take me. You can't. I have until morning!"

"That's true for the others, dear."

"I'm not your dear!"

"But exceptions must be made when it's possible to place a child with a relative."

And that, at last, stopped her.

A relative. For a moment, hope filled April's chest, swelling up like a balloon. She had a mother, but more importantly, April had an *uncle*. And he'd come for her.

"He came?" April asked.

"He's in here."

The woman gestured to a room off the entryway, and April pushed past her, running, yelling, "Gabriel! You—"

"Hello, April."

April knew the voice. Even before she turned, long before she saw him, she wanted to close her eyes and shake her head—like an Etch A Sketch, she wanted to wipe the last five minutes away, clear the slate and go back to the way it was.

"You're not Gabriel." She took a step backward and didn't let herself think about how foolish she sounded.

She didn't even let herself get angry when the man laughed and said, "No. I'm not."

"April, this is your father!" Tiny-Pencil Lady threw out her arms and decreed, like April had won some kind of contest—like this was some kind of game. "There was a DNA test. We have a court order. Everything's already set."

"DNA test?" April said.

"Straw." Reggie shrugged. "We all got drinks at the sweet shop, remember? I might have stolen yours. Except it was trash at that point. Does it count as stealing if it's trash? I don't know."

He sounded nervous. He looked almost scared. But April was terrified because this virtual stranger was standing there telling her that he was her father when April absolutely, positively did not have one of those.

Then something started to change inside of April, like

when your hands are freezing cold and only start to hurt as they warm back up. Her whole body was starting to burn.

And when the woman said, "We can get you out of here and back with your family today," April caught fire.

"No."

"What do you mean, no?" Tiny-Pencil Lady actually laughed, like it was funny or absurd or April was playing a joke.

"No. There's been some kind of mistake. I'm with my family."

"I'm sure it feels like your friends are your family, but April—" She leaned close and smiled big and kept talking, but there was a whirling sound inside of April's head. It was like she was back in the museum. Like the room was about to go whoosh and the fire was going to spread.

"No. No. I don't have a father," she said because she didn't. "You mean my uncle. I have an uncle."

"You may have an uncle as well." The woman laughed.

"You're probably wondering how," Reggie prompted, "I recognized you. Or . . . I thought I did. When I saw the picture in the paper, it was one thing. But then when I saw you in person . . . April, I would know you anywhere. You haven't changed since you were a baby. I mean, you're bigger." He held up his hands to illustrate, as if she might not know what the word *bigger* meant. "I knew you, April. I knew you were my daughter. And so . . ."

"Straw," April finished for him.

"Straw." He smiled.

"And we have the DNA test to prove it." Ms. Pitts didn't pick up her tiny pencil, but it was very much implied. "Now you're free to go along with your father, dear."

Father.

Her father was holding out a hand. Her father was leading her toward the door. And when April screamed. When she bolted for the stairs. When she kicked and cried and tried to claw her way back into her old life, it was her father who carried her out into the cold, dark night.

TWENTY-SEVEN

I'm so sorry, April," the stranger said. But he wasn't sorry for the right things. If he had been, he would have told the driver to turn that fancy car around. He would have taken her back to her friends. He would have taken her home.

Except April didn't have a home. Not anymore. And when she thought about the look in Gabriel's eyes, she had to wonder if she ever had.

"Oh no. Is your lip quivering? It is. You're gonna cry, aren't you? Please don't cry. I don't want you to cry," Reggie said. "Geez. This is rough. I almost want to take you back now."

"Then do it," April snapped, and he looked like a puppy that had just been kicked.

"I can't do that, April. You're the most important thing in the world to me."

"I don't know anything about you!"

"Sure you do," he said. "I'm Reggie Dupree. I like toffee and chocolate chip cookies. Ten years ago, my wife and daughter disappeared. And I've been looking for them every day since. Hey." He shifted on the leather seat as if to see her better. "We're gonna see your friends. We might even . . . I mean, they might not want to . . . but maybe they can come live with us, too? How does that sound?"

It sounded amazing and too good to be true, which meant it probably was.

She turned back to the window and watched as the car drove down the shore, past icy rocks and whitecaps breaking on the cold, dark water that stretched all the way to the horizon.

"He didn't try to save me, did he?"

"Save you?"

"Keep me. He didn't want me."

"Ahhh. *Gabriel*. Honestly? I don't know about him." She felt a warm hand land on her cold one and squeeze just once. "But I want you more than anything on this earth."

And the one thing April knew for sure was that he wasn't lying.

"You really are my dad, aren't you?"

For a second, he just looked shocked. And then he laughed. "Well . . . yeah. From this point on, kiddo. You're stuck with me." He squeezed her hand again, then dug around in a little compartment and pulled out a bottle of water and handed it to her. "Here. You like water? I mean, everyone likes water. It's . . . you know . . . water. But maybe you don't like it. I guess there's a lot we don't know about each other, huh?"

That was the understatement of the century, but April was thirsty, so she opened the bottle and took a big drink. And then another. By the time she was finished, she'd found the courage to say, "Tell me about my mother."

He only faltered a moment before asking, "What about her?"

"Anything. Everything. How did you meet?"

"We went to school together. Or, well, we did from the time she was fifteen or so. She'd had an accident, they said.

Her family was gone. I was kind of a screwup, but she was a natural at everything. Pretty much everyone at school was either in love with her or terrified of her. Sometimes both at once."

"What do you know about her?"

"Honestly?" He leaned his head back against the soft leather. "I'm not sure I ever knew her at all. But when I think about her, all I can remember is . . . fear. She was afraid. All the time. She said her uncle was trying to kill her. She always said that. At first, I thought it was kind of a joke — something she made up. I mean no one goes around talking about their murderous uncle if they actually *have* a murderous uncle. But then I found out about the nightmares. Nightmares you can't make up." He turned and watched the city pass by the window, neon lights on cold, wet streets. "You don't want to hear all this."

"Try me," April dared, and he talked on.

"When we had you, I thought she might calm down, but if anything, she got worse. And then one day there was a story on the news about Gabriel Winterborne going missing. The next day you were both just . . . gone. I thought you were dead. I thought I'd never see you again."

He reached for April again, but April flinched and

pulled away. A brief flash of hurt crossed his face before he forced a grin.

"You want a pony? I can buy you a pony. That was a joke, by the way. Unless you want one, and then I can totally make that happen. World's Greatest Dad right here. Just you wait. You're gonna want to buy me a mug and everything."

"I don't want a pony. I want my friends. And my life back. I want . . ." Gabriel. April wanted Gabriel. And Smithers and Izzy and to go to sleep to the sound of Violet's snoring and to be woken up by some kind of SadieMatic. "I want to go home. I finally had a home," she said so softly he might not have even heard it.

But he wasn't insulted. He wasn't even hurt. He was just . . . resigned.

"I know, kiddo. Hey, do you still climb?"

April didn't know why the question stopped her. But it did. He shook his head and threw his head back against the seat like he'd just had a memory that was one of his top five favorites.

"Man, you used to climb everything. There wasn't a crib in the world that could hold you. Those little play-pen things? Forget about it. You could get out of car seats, too. We couldn't turn our backs for a minute. I swear, you climbed before you walked. You weren't afraid of heights. You weren't afraid of *anything*." He looked at her and, suddenly, he wasn't smiling anymore. "I'm sorry, April. I'm sorry I wasn't there for you. I'm sorry I couldn't keep the fear away. That was my job. And all I want in the whole world is the chance to do better from now on."

It was a pretty speech from a handsome man in a fancy car, but April would have traded it all for a life in the cold, drafty cellars beneath Winterborne House. Not because she needed Gabriel, but because Gabriel was the first person who had ever needed her.

When the car slowed and stopped, a big man opened April's door, but April didn't budge.

"This isn't your house," she said even though Reggie probably could have figured that out for himself. They were parked right by the shore on the outskirts of the city.

"Oh yeah," Reggie said. "That's not my only house. I'm kind of loaded," he admitted with a shrug.

"I want to call my friends."

"Of course you do. And you will once we get there."

"Get where?"

"Not sure yet. Italy, maybe. I've got a place in Scotland. Hey, have you ever been to Iceland? I hear Iceland's cool."

Everything inside of April went still in that moment. Her heart stopped beating, and her mind stopped thinking, and her veins were full of ice as he said, "You're gonna have to trust me, chickadee."

And then her blood turned to fire. She remembered her mother's tortured, fevered dreams—the soundtrack of her nightmare: *You don't get to miss twice, chickadee.*

April was getting out of the car. April was running. She didn't know why. And she didn't know where. She just knew that, suddenly, her arms were too heavy. She couldn't even feel her hands. And her legs were like noodles that had been cooked way too long.

She didn't know how she ended up on the ground, the empty water bottle beside her. It was like the museum and the fire, as April watched a figure swoop down through the haze and lift her up, but this time she wanted to fight. She needed to fight.

But she was far too woozy and sleepy to try.

TWENTY-EIGHT

WHAT WOULD SADIE DO?

April didn't know what was worse: the headache, the bellyache, or the sudden spike of fear that hit her as soon as she realized that she didn't know where she was. She didn't know *when* she was.

She was lying on a big, plush bed with way too many pillows. There was a dresser and a chair and a bathroom. The walls were an expensive-looking wood, and the ceiling wasn't all that high. But the weirdest thing about the little room was simple: it was moving. Either that or April was about to be very, very sick.

Maybe both, she thought as she pushed herself upright on the bed. The curtains were swinging like a pendulum, and April had to hold on to the dresser to find her balance.

She had to keep one hand on the wall as she made her way to the window.

"Please be wrong. Please be wrong. Please be—"

She wasn't wrong.

April gasped, and her warm breath fogged against the chilly glass as she looked out at the huge white moon and inky black waves that turned frothy white as she sliced through the water.

On a boat.

They were at sea.

And they were moving very, very quickly.

The boat rocked and creaked and almost threw April off her feet. The water was too rough to be going so quickly, but someone had decided it was worth the risk, and April didn't have to wonder who. Or why.

She should have felt panic or fear or at least a little bit of seasickness. But April never did what she was supposed to do.

She certainly didn't stay in rooms she didn't want to be in. Even if the doors were locked. No one lives with Sadie Marie Simmons without learning a whole new appreciation for bobby pins and good old-fashioned elbow grease, and soon April was pushing out into a hallway made of more of that shiny wood.

She heard voices, though she couldn't make out the words. Then a door slammed and April jumped back into her little bedroom and closed the door just in time to hear someone pass outside.

As soon as the coast was clear, she eased back into the hallway and down the stairs.

A sign warned **CREW ONLY**, but April wasn't going to let a sign tell her what to do. She had to find a radio or a computer. She had to find some way to call for help or signal to land. At the very least, she had to figure out where the heck she was and how long they'd been going. She knew in her gut that she was a long, long way from Winterborne House, but she would have jumped overboard and swum for it if she'd thought that would work.

(It wouldn't have worked.)

So April just kept creeping down that forbidden hallway. When she reached a wide metal door, she stopped. And listened. But all she heard was silence.

So, of course, she pulled out her bobby pin and went to work, a kind of To Do list taking shape in her mind.

Step one: unlock door.

A moment later, the lock clicked and April pushed inside, a thin sliver of light growing wider in the darkness.

Step two: find a light.

April flipped a switch and blinked as a fluorescent bulb came flickering to life, buzzing and humming as April took in a room full of ropes and shelves of supplies.

And a woman tied to a chair.

Step three: wake up the woman who, evidently, gave birth to you but then abandoned you but, given the circumstances, might have had her reasons.

April closed the door, then crept closer. "Hey, uh . . . Georgia." Carefully, she reached out and shook her shoulder. She wanted to cry with relief when she felt the woman's warm skin and knew for sure that she was breathing.

"Georgia," she said, a little louder this time. "Wake up. Georgia!" April screamed as quietly as she could, and then she felt her throat burn. Her eyes watered, and when she said, "Mom?" her voice actually broke. Along with the rest of her.

Because the woman wasn't waking up. Her head hung lifeless, and April couldn't forget that — not too long before — she'd been stabbed and shot and who knew what else. Maybe she'd never wake up. Maybe —

"You called me Mom."

She was alive. She was awake. And, for the first time since April had known her, she might have been smiling. Maybe. Well, at least she was scowling less.

So April said, "Yeah, well, I was desperate."

"I won't tell anyone."

"Thanks," April told her.

"I'll probably be dead before I get the chance."

April wanted her to be joking—teasing. She wanted to know that sarcasm was hereditary. She wanted to hear her mother laugh, but Georgia only snapped, "Well, are you gonna cut me loose or let me die here?"

"Don't know." April backed up a step, just for good measure. "Still thinking about it."

"Think faster," Georgia ordered, but then a light seemed to go on behind her eyes. "You're still wondering if I'm the villain or the heroine of this story, aren't you?" April didn't lie and didn't nod and didn't move, and her mother absolutely, positively didn't smile when she said, "Oh, sweetheart, someday you'll realize . . . *I'm both*."

"Yeah. Well." April swallowed. "I guess that's just math."

April was suddenly so tired. She wanted to blame it on whatever had been in that bottle of water to knock her out, but she knew it was more than that. She was tired of running. She was tired of waiting. She was tired of missing a mother who would never, ever be what April had always wanted. But maybe this was the mother she needed.

"When the museum burned," she said slowly, "how did I get out?"

The boat rocked and the light buzzed, but it was like the whole world stood still as April's mother said, "I carried you."

And then April got to work, looking around for a knife or some scissors to cut through the rope or the tape, but there wasn't rope or tape. There were chains.

"You're literally chained to that chair! Seriously?"

"My reputation precedes me." Georgia sounded almost smug. But that didn't make her any less chained to a chair.

April looked around, then studied the chair; maybe the chains could slide off with April's help. Maybe she could disassemble the chair itself? Her little bobby pin wasn't going to work against that giant lock, but there had to be a way! So she searched the shelves. She didn't see any bolt cutters, but there was a crowbar. Maybe April could find the proverbial weak link. Or . . . was that liquid nitrogen?

April zeroed in on the little container and asked herself, "What would Sadie do?"

"What would—Oh boy," Georgia said when April picked up the liquid nitrogen and began to pour.

A foggy white cloud billowed up and a sizzling sound like bacon filled the air.

"April—"

"I've got—"

"The door!" Georgia snapped, and, for the first time, April heard the voices.

The men were back. The men were out there. She crept to the door and turned the lock as quietly as she could. But the men had the key, she remembered a split second later when the lock turned again.

The door opened.

At first, they seemed confused to find April locked in the wrong room—like maybe their minds were playing tricks on them.

"What are you . . ." one of them started, but he didn't finish. Instead, he pounced. April ducked and ran beneath his arms. She picked up the crowbar and hurled it as hard as she could. It flew over one of the men's heads and hit the back of the chair with a bang, and the largest of the two men smirked. "Missed."

And April's mind flashed back to another night—another fight.

"Meant to," she said just as the brittle chain fractured into a million pieces. In the next moment, Georgia Winterborne was rising like a phoenix from the chair.

The ends of the chain were like long, deadly tentacles in her hands—lashing and flying and swirling around the room until the men were bloody, unconscious heaps on the floor.

"Come on." Georgia wasn't shocked or stunned or even a little bit out of breath. "We've got to get out of here."

"No!" April didn't know what she was saying—what she was doing—until she was standing between the woman with the chains and the doorway. "Just tell me . . . Why?"

Georgia looked at her like she was realizing for the first time that she'd given birth to an idiot.

"Because they're gonna bury me at sea if we stay here."

"No. Why did you . . . I mean, what did I do to make

you . . ." It was the thing April had wondered for her whole life, but she couldn't even get the question out. And, in the end, she didn't have to.

"You thought I didn't want you." Georgia looked like it was the first time such a thing had ever crossed her mind.

"Of course you didn't want me! I just never knew why. Exactly. But, you know what, never mind. It doesn't matter." April was stupid for asking. Stupid for caring. Stupid in every possible way.

She went to the door and was trying to move the heavy leg of one of the unconscious men when she heard, "When I was fifteen, my uncle Evert hired someone to blow up our family's boat."

"I know that part," April snapped.

"When I woke up, there were burns all over my body. It took months before I could bend my leg. I couldn't remember anything except a loud noise and a white light and then just nothing. I'm not sure how long I slept. I wasn't sure where I was—just that it was cold. It was always so cold. They told me my family was dead and my home wasn't safe and I was alone in the world. *I was alone.*" The last words were barely a whisper.

"Where were you?" April asked. "Who were they? Why didn't you come for Gabriel? How—"

"Gabriel was dead! They were all dead! I was the last of the Winterbornes, and I was never going to be safe unless . . ." She shook her head like even the memory was physically painful. "I was at a school. An . . . institute. They said they could . . . teach me."

"Teach you what?"

"To take care of myself. To get revenge on Evert. To be someone else. We should be going, April. We don't have time for—"

"I've waited ten years for this!" April said, too loudly. "Is he really my father?"

She had the look of a woman who wished she could remember how to lie when she said, "Yes. I didn't know who they were. What *he* was. I didn't know . . ."

"Who were they?"

"The people who set the bomb," she said with a shrug. "Evidently Evert hired the best. When I found out, I ran. They were looking for a woman and a baby, you see. They were never going to stop looking for a woman and a baby. So . . . it seemed like the best way to keep you safe. From

Reggie. From Evert. From the Institute. The world was hunting Winterbornes. So I didn't leave you. I *hid* you. Do you understand?" Then she gave a very Winterborne-y growl and snapped, "And then you had to go and fall off a balcony."

And that shut April right up.

Georgia opened the door, and when she spoke again, it was a whisper. "Stay close. Stay quiet. Don't be stupid."

And April couldn't help but ask, "What if I go two out of three?"

TWENTY-NINE

WORST. REUNION. EVER.

Doesn't matter how fancy a yacht is, it's going to look more like a fortress than a palace if you have to skulk around the halls with a woman with chains in her hands, or so April told herself as they crept down the hall, then up some stairs. They were closer to the outside then. She could feel it in the cold, wet air. And, more than anything, April wanted to be outside. To be in the fresh air and free, but Georgia stopped and glared down at April.

"When we get out there, you have to do what I say."

"Um . . . okay?"

"No matter *what* I say. You have to do it *when* I say it. No questions. No arguing. When I talk, you act. Do you understand me?"

It seemed pretty late to be playing such an obvious Mom card. There had been a time when April might have longed for such a thing, but that window had closed. She'd stopped waiting and looking and longing for a mother months ago. All that ever came of that was heartbreak.

"April! Promise me." She didn't feel like April's mom, but she sounded like Gabriel's sister. And, so far, the Winterbornes had proven pretty good at keeping April alive.

"Yeah. Sure. I promise."

"Stay low. Move quickly. Move quietly."

"Move *where?*" April asked, but it was too late; Georgia was already out the door and sweeping across the deck like a ghost.

April wasn't nearly so graceful. Giant waves crashed against the hull, and the yacht sliced through the icy water that seemed to be trying with all its might to push them back to land.

She stumbled and teetered and grabbed on to the railing, rushing as quickly and as quietly as she could in the wake of the figure that was nothing more than a shadow.

April's eyes were just starting to adjust to the dark when

Georgia crouched low on the deck and motioned toward a lifeboat that dangled on the other side of the rail.

"This is our ride," she whispered. "Get in."

It wasn't April's promise that kept her from arguing. It was her commitment to getting the heck out of there that made her climb over the railing and drop down into the boat on the other side.

"Come on," April told the woman just as there was a subtle click in the darkness. Light flooded the deck, bearing down on the two of them. April threw a hand over her eyes and almost fell out of the boat, but there was no missing the voice that said, "Oh man, I was really hoping I wasn't going to have to do this."

April couldn't move—couldn't breathe—because Reggie Dupree wasn't smiling anymore.

"April, go to your room. I need to have a talk with your mother."

And in spite of the cold wind and the rough seas and even the man with the gun, April had to laugh, because that was her father. Talking about her mother. But they weren't a family. And they never would be.

"If I say no, do I still get a pony?"

"Maybe, sweetie," he said, because he obviously wasn't very good at being the bad guy. Or, more likely, he was just terrible at being a father. But that didn't matter, because April was never going to win Daughter of the Year.

The lifeboat was rocking, and if anything, it felt like the yacht was going faster. Or maybe the seas were just rougher. Icy cold sprays blew up, striking her in the face, and her hair was wet and dripping in her eyes. Or maybe she was just crying. Surely she wasn't crying.

"Don't make me," she said, but she wasn't sure if she was talking to the man or the woman, her father or her mother. "Please. Please don't make me."

They'd been literal feet away from freedom. They were still so close. Reggie was on the other side of the deck, and the yacht was moving quickly, rocking and swaying. He'd get a shot off, sure, but what were the chances it'd miss? A lot better than their chances if they stayed.

So she looked at her mother and pleaded, "Please."

But Georgia said, "You made me a promise."

And April knew. She just knew.

"Mom!" she screamed, but Georgia was hitting a switch and saying, "I love you. Don't look back," and then April was flying through the air, falling, plummeting, then hitting the water with an icy splash. The little lifeboat landed in the wake of the giant yacht that was still moving too fast on the rough waves, farther and farther and farther away.

And suddenly, April was right back where she'd always been: alone, abandoned, and completely on her own.

THIRTY

THE NIGHT THE WATER BURNED

The boat was small and the ocean was big and the lights of the yacht were disappearing into the distance. They'd come back for her eventually, she knew. Reggie wanted her. He might have even needed her. So for the first time in her life, she told herself that her *father* was going to return for her someday.

And that was a very, very, very bad thing.

The only light was from the full moon, and the air felt like a freezer. The storm was over, but the waves were high, and in the tiny boat, April thought she might be sick. She told herself it was the motion of the waves, but she knew better. The water could have been as smooth as glass, and April would have felt like hanging her head over the side and losing what little food was in her stomach. But she needed that food. That was her last food. So she sat there, surrounded by darkness and cold.

And probably sharks.

Man, she hoped there weren't sharks.

She wanted to yell, but she didn't dare risk it, half afraid that her mother wouldn't hear her. Half afraid that her father would. But mostly April was terrified that neither would bother to care.

Not that it mattered. They'd be back. Reggie and his thugs would kill Georgia, and then they'd be back for April.

Which, when compared to the sharks, April wasn't sure what was worse.

And then a sound came screaming across the water —a massive roar followed by a ball of flames shooting into the sky. She could have sworn she felt the explosion on the waves, a ripple effect that would be coursing through her for the rest of her life as she watched the yacht explode.

She was too far away to feel the heat, but she felt like she might catch fire anyway. Because the truth hit her. She was alone. Again. Abandoned by her mother. Again. Set adrift on the sea of life. Again.

It should have felt comfortable. Like a second skin. But all April felt was cold. And fear.

Everybody knows about the Winterbornes. That one morning, long ago, a perfect family went out on their perfect boat for a perfect day upon the water. Everyone knows there was a terrible storm and a tragic accident and, eventually, an explosion so big that even the water caught fire.

Everyone knows that the sole survivor was a little boy, who floated on the sea for hours, cold and afraid, injured and alone. The last of the Winterbornes.

Nobody knew the truth.

And as April sat in that tiny lifeboat, she realized no one ever would. After all, April was a Winterborne. And absolutely no one would ever know what happened to her.

So she kept her gaze trained on the horizon as the fire faded and her eyes adjusted to the dark black night that was filled with about a million billion stars. April felt like she could see every single one—maybe count them. She had the time, she realized. People counted sheep to go to sleep. She might as well count stars while she waited to die.

Except April didn't want to die.

April wanted to be looking up at the Winterborne crest

woven into the canopy of her big, soft bed. She wished she were listening to Violet's snores instead of the waves lapping at the side of the boat.

April wanted to survive. But there were no oars in the boat. No sail and no motor, and so she was at the mercy of the currents to take her home. Because April finally knew where home was. But she didn't know where north was. The moon was directly overhead, and it would be hours until sunrise. By then, April feared, it might be too late, because the ocean was vast and empty and April was the only girl in the world.

She leaned over the side of the boat and tried to row with her hands, but the water was too cold. The mainland was too far. And there wasn't a thing April could do but cry and pray.

Was this what Gabriel had felt like? Was this what her mother would remember, if she could remember anything at all? Maybe this was some kind of terrible Winterborne family tradition. If so, April didn't want to be a Winterborne anymore. She'd never wanted to be a Winterborne in the first place! She'd just wanted to be loved. And look how that had turned out.

She didn't even have her mother's key.

So she closed her eyes and leaned her head back on the side of the boat and listened as her heart got louder and the rest of the world got quieter. Soon, there was nothing but the lapping waves and the subtle thump, thump, thump of . . . wait. That wasn't her heart.

She shot upright and looked over the side of the little boat at the smoldering rubble that filled the water, stretching out like a string of fire on the waves.

It was like a path, a road. And right then, April knew she had to go in the *opposite* direction—away from the burning wreckage and back to land. Back to her friends. Back to home.

So she reached into the icy water and pulled out a blackened board. Then she took her makeshift oar and started to row away from the fire and the ghosts.

THIRTY-ONE

RETURN TO WINTERBORNE ISLAND

At first April thought it was a mirage. Or a dream. Or maybe just a product of her very tired, very active imagination. But as soon as she saw the rickety pier, she knew there was no way her subconscious would conjure something so likely to scrape her knee and give her tetanus.

Besides, April knew that pier. She knew that island. And a little part of April knew it wasn't home, but it was the next best thing. So she rowed harder until she could tie up the little lifeboat and then crawl out and pick her way across the rotting boards. She fell through twice and scraped her ankle once, but soon she was crashing to her knees on the rocky beach and looking at the outline of the trees.

There was shelter through those trees. There might have been food. And water. Maybe even a radio or a way to call for help. But there were also a whole bunch of snares, holes, traps, and tripwires. And April tripped over everything, so she sat there for a long time, trying to work up the courage to move. Or maybe just the desperation.

She could build a signal fire. Maybe just sit there on the nice, hard rocks until help came. But *would* help come? Would anybody ever come looking for her? Would they know she was missing?

Would they even care?

Her breath was just starting to return to normal when she saw the light. She heard the voices. And then her heart started pounding again for entirely different reasons as she crept over the rocks and looked around the bend. The men must not have known about the rickety pier, because they were dragging a raft up onto the rocks and staggering out of the icy surf. Wet. Bloody.

And suddenly April knew there was something far worse than being stuck on the island alone.

Slowly, she stood and tried to ease away, but the rocks were slick and uneven, and her foot slid. Her ankle turned.

She cried out in pain. And one of the men shouted, "Over there!"

After that, April forgot all about her twisted ankle and took off, running for the trees.

Shouts echoed in the night.

Bullets ricocheted off of stones, and April ducked. She'd just had time to think, *Well, at least it can't get any worse,* when another man yelled, "You idiot! We need her alive!"

And April had to admit, *Nope. That's probably worse.*

As soon as she reached the shelter of the trees, she paused to catch her breath and get her bearings. But everything was so dark. And April was so tired. She couldn't see the stars or the moon. She couldn't remember if this was the path to the cabin. She couldn't even tell if she was on a path at all. The brush was so thick, and the trees were so tall. Sadie would have known where to go, but Sadie was a million miles away and April couldn't think about that. Not then. Not there.

"This way," someone yelled, and April heard movement through the trees. Soon, men were crashing through the thick brush, and from that point on, she didn't even try to be quiet; she just ran, her eyes adjusting to the dim light, looking for signs. And when she saw one, she didn't hesitate, she jumped.

A minute later she heard the snap and crash that comes when a two-hundred-pound man doesn't jump over a trip-wire, and then April did the only thing she could.

She ran faster.

And faster. Until her lungs burned and her hands shook. She wanted to be sick, except she didn't dare slow down. Part of her thought she should stop and hide. And another part of her thought she should run faster — maybe loop around and go back to the beach. Their boat must have had a motor. That was the only way they'd reached her so fast. If she could get back to the beach, unseen . . . If she could just get to that boat . . .

Then maybe she could head away from the rising sun and back to the mainland.

Then maybe April could go home.

But which way was the beach? She stopped and turned and tried to get her bearings. And that was when she heard it: silence.

There was no more running, no more crashing or

cursing. There was nothing but the pounding of April's heart and her own ragged breath until . . .

The trees moved. A branch rustled. April had no idea how they'd gotten in front of her, but someone had; she was certain.

So she picked up a rock and crept toward the bushes.

And then arms were around her again, pulling her close and squeezing her tight. And Reggie's voice was in her ear, saying, "April, sweetheart, you don't have to run away from—Ow!"

Swordplay, a person learned from Gabriel Winterborne. Biting, April had learned on her own.

"You didn't have to do that!" he snapped.

"Tell that to the guys who shot at me."

"I did, honey. I told them. And then I killed them."

He'd killed them.

He'd killed them.

He'd . . .

"See? April, sweetheart?" He took her by the shoulders and turned her so that he could look into her eyes. "Are you okay? Are you hurt? I know you don't believe it right now, but I'm on your side. You can trust me."

But April didn't trust anyone. Or she hadn't, not for ten years. That was how she'd survived. That was how she'd made it from home to home, disappointment to disappointment.

"Now, tell me, are you hurt?" He smoothed her hair away from her face like he was a real dad. Like he really cared. And that was how she knew he was lying.

"Sweetheart, you have to believe me."

"Maybe I don't want to," April said, and then she kicked and bit and broke away, ducking through the trees and leaping over rocks, but he was still back there.

And she was . . . you know . . . still *on an island*. If only she could lose him . . . If only she could get to the beach and the boats . . .

If only . . .

"April, get back here! Now!" he snapped like he was the boss of her. Like he was . . . her father. "April, please?" He tried again. "Please let me explain. I don't know what your mother told you," Reggie called into the night. "But I'm sure it's not true."

And April couldn't help herself, she shouted back, "She said the people you work for killed her whole family."

And then, suddenly, he stopped running.

"I always wondered why she left." He actually seemed sad when he said it, and April realized that she wasn't the only one who had been left behind with no explanation, only to spend ten years wondering exactly where it all went wrong. "She didn't have to run. She didn't have to take you. She could have . . ."

"What? Hung around so you could finish her off like the rest of the Winterbornes?"

"I would never hurt your mother!" She heard him moving through the trees. "Just like I'd never hurt you."

"Is she dead?" April had sworn she was going to be quiet, but she couldn't help herself. She had to know.

"I don't know," he confessed. "That's the truth. She went over the side. It was dark. But we'll find her, April. We'll search for her as soon as the sun's up and then we'll be okay. We'll be a family again." April squeezed her eyes shut and willed herself not to cry, because there were some lies that were only okay to tell yourself. "We'll get off the grid, and this time we'll disappear *together*. You want that, right? Our family? I want that. I've already missed too much. The last time I saw you, I could carry you with one hand. You were such a cute baby. Do you still burp when you laugh?"

April hated how much a part of her wanted to hear these stories. She'd never known her first word or when she'd taken her first steps. He might have a photo album full of baby pictures somewhere, a tiny chest full of tiny clothes. In some small way, a small part of April might have been normal. Once. But it died a long, long time ago.

"I just want to take you home," he called out.

"I have a home!"

"You have an illusion!" He didn't yell. He roared. "Who's going to keep you safe? Gabriel Winterborne? He's no match for them, sweetheart. He'll get hurt. Your friends will get hurt. Everyone you love will get hurt because they want your mother. They'll want you. And after this, they'll want me too. I am your only chance. I can teach you. The way I was taught. The way your mother was taught. I can keep you safe!" And when he spoke again, his voice cracked. "Please, April, the only thing I've ever wanted was to keep you safe."

He was lying. He had to be lying.

The sun was starting to come up, and even in the forest, April could see the little rays of light breaking through. She could make out the bushes. The rocks. The sparring dummies hanging by ropes in the trees. The targets with old knives. Old swords.

Soon she'd be able to see where she was going. But *he'd* be able to see *her,* so whatever she was going to do, she had to do it soon.

"But we can get away now. We can be together. We can be a family."

"I have a family!" April shouted. And for the first time in her life, it was true.

"Do you want to take them with you? The other kids? We can do that. If they want to come—"

"They don't."

The voice came out of the thick brush and speck-led light, and at first, April didn't know what she was hearing—what she was seeing. But then something—*someone*—flew off a ledge and landed on Reggie, knock-ing him to the ground.

"Tim! What are you—"

"Run now, question later, love." Colin darted out of the bushes and grabbed April's hand, and April didn't have to be told twice. They took off through the trees. Branches hit her in the face. Thorny bushes snagged her clothes, but nothing could slow April down.

"What are you doing here?" she asked, because she'd always been good at multitasking.

"Duh. We're kidnapping you back! We're re-knapping you."

"But . . . how?"

"Tracker in your pocket," Colin said.

She heard Tim running along behind them, catching up.

"You slipped a tracker in my pocket?"

"Not us, love. Gabriel."

Then April stumbled. She thought about how Gabriel had knelt on the foyer floor, forcing her into a coat, practically strangling her with a scarf. At the moment, it had felt like he was bundling her up to send her away, but now it felt like he was wrapping her up because she was precious and he wanted to keep her safe. She slipped a hand in her pocket and came out with a SadieSonic.

"She added GPS," Tim said. "Now, go!" And they took off.

"Booby trap in three—two—*jump!*" April said, and they soared over a tripwire, but she winced and stumbled, landing on her bad ankle, and then Tim was behind her, hand on her back.

"Keep going."

But that one little hesitation was too much. A shot rang out, and, in front of them, a branch splintered. They skidded to a stop.

"You know, April, I really thought we had a few years before you started sneaking around with boys. Now I've got to play the Dad card and be all, *Tim, Colin, have her home by eleven*." He was teasing. He was joking. He actually laughed like he was so funny. "Guys, relax. I'm not the villain here."

"Yeah. Um. Pretty sure you are." April glanced at the gun, and he seemed to realize it was still in his hand.

"Oh, geez!" He lowered the weapon and looked her in the eye. "I'm so sorry about that. I wouldn't hurt you, April. I would never hurt any of you." He waved at Tim and Colin. "Hi, Tim, Colin. Nice to see you again. Wanna come live with us? There's some debate as to where, but at the moment, we're leaning toward Iceland."

"April . . ." Colin sounded confused and very, very leery.

"I think we'd rather go back to Winterborne House . . . uh . . . Dad?" April tried, and it kinda sorta worked because a huge grin spread across his face.

"Wow. That was cool. You were talking when you

left, but it was more like Dadadada—which was super cute! But that . . . wow. I've waited a long time to hear that." He actually wiped his eyes. (With the hand that wasn't holding the gun.) "I wasn't lying, you know. When I said I was a screwup at school. But I was always good at loving you."

What would April's life have been like if her mother hadn't left, hadn't run, hadn't hidden her away without a trace? Who would she have been if anyone had ever cared about her even a tiny little bit? But she would never know, so she'd tried to never care.

"It's true, you know. I'm really *not* the villain." Reggie sounded so sincere that for a second even April wondered if she might be crazy enough to believe him. "But I can't let you go back."

"If you love me, you will."

"Then who's gonna keep you safe?"

"I will," a voice said. The trees moved. Except it wasn't the trees. It was a coat made out of other coats, brown and black and green, draping and sweeping, almost hiding the long, silver blade that was catching bits and pieces of the rising sun.

Gabriel said, "Get out of here."

Reggie cocked his head. "Well, you didn't ask very nicely."

"Wasn't talking to you." With that, Gabriel circled Reggie like a predator circles prey. "I said go," he snapped at the kids, but April was frozen, too terrified to move.

"Thanks for taking good care of my girl, but I'll be taking it from here," Reggie said while Gabriel circled.

"She's not your girl."

"Yes! She is! And if you care about her even a little bit, you'll get out of our way and wish us well."

"Not gonna let you take her."

"Not asking!" Reggie snapped. Then he seemed to recall something because he huffed and said, "I was sorry to hear about your uncle Evert. He was a real good customer."

The words were meant to enrage Gabriel, throw him off his game and make him lose his cool. They worked. He lunged at Reggie, but his balance was off and his usual grace was gone. Something was wrong, and Reggie skittered away, unharmed. Then April remembered the fall. The dislocated shoulder. And the fact that she'd never seen him fight with just one hand.

"Look, man," Reggie said. "I don't want to hurt you. You're family!"

"I'm not your family."

"No. See . . . you're related to April. I'm related to April. So we're . . . Never mind." Then he raised a hand. "Hey. I just remembered. I have this."

It happened in slow motion. And it happened in a flash. Both of those things couldn't possibly have been true. But they were. Because one moment she was watching Gabriel's sword slice through the air. The next, Reggie's gun was up and his bullet was slicing right through Gabriel's good arm.

He stumbled. He faltered. The sword tumbled from his grasp, landing beside a little stack of stones, but he never stopped moving. And he never fell. He just kept coming, fighting, until Reggie pushed him away with a shove, and they circled each other once again. Two trained men who weren't going to give up until one or the other was dead.

"You're a tough one," Reggie said, breathing hard. "How about him? How tough is he?" Then he pointed the gun at Tim.

Gone was the guy who'd bought them candy, the man who'd teared up when she'd called him Dad. And for the first time, April had absolutely no doubt why Georgia ran away, leaving her baby and her key and disappearing into the wind.

April didn't realize she was shouting, "No!" until she found herself between Tim and the gun. She just knew she had to. She knew it in her bones because April had always been good at protecting what was hers. For years, all she'd had was herself. But that wasn't true anymore.

"I'll go!" she shouted.

"April, no!" someone screamed.

"I'll go with you," she blurted. "Just put the gun down. Just don't hurt anyone else, Mr. Dupree."

There was hurt in his voice and his eyes. "April, I'm your dad."

He started toward her, and April stepped back. "No." Her voice cracked. "No, you're not my dad."

"Yes, I—" But he never finished. He threw open his arms, and April stepped aside. She pushed. And then she watched as he tripped over the little stack of rocks and fell into a giant hole, crashing into the blackness.

Then April looked down at the man in the bottom of the pit, howling and writhing in pain, and said, "I already have one."

THIRTY-TWO

THE GUEST

Morning came. And with it, bright sun and clear air and a feeling like April had never known before: Hope. Happiness. And more than a little bit of hunger. But that last part was only temporary, she realized, as they pushed through the doors of Winterborne House and smelled bacon on the air even though it was almost noon.

"Ooh, Sadie and Violet are my favorites!" Colin exclaimed, then took off running for the kitchen.

But April didn't follow.

"Gabriel?" She looked back at him. The hospital had said the bullet only grazed him. They'd stitched him up and given him some painkillers and a sling and sent him home with instructions to come back in a week and get it looked at.

"Does it hurt?" she asked for about the millionth time.

"Not as much as my pride."

"You put a tracker in my pocket," she blurted, because she was an idiot sometimes and idiots say idiotic things just so they can stop thinking them.

But the weirdest thing happened. Gabriel actually smirked. *A smirk!* A real one. It wasn't a full-fledged smile, but it was a start. "Of course I did," he said. "It doesn't matter who comes for you, April. I'm always going to get you back."

She felt her cheeks go red. "You're just saying that because I'm your niece."

But the smile faded then, into sadness mixed with confusion. "I'm saying that because you're my girl."

And then April's eyes were burning because eyes did that sometimes.

That was just science.

"I'll make you a deal, April. I won't leave you if you won't leave me." Gabriel winced and sank down in a chair, but it was the look in his eye that told April that a bullet wound was the least of his problems. "Turns out, I'm not good at being left behind."

"Izzy will be back soon," April said. "I know it."

But Gabriel didn't say anything for a long, long time.

"Is this how she felt? All those years I was . . . away? Did she feel like this?"

"I don't know," April said.

"I need to know she's safe."

"She is. She's fine. We'd know it if she wasn't."

He huffed. "My own sister was alive for twenty years, and I didn't have a clue, so forgive me if I'm not optimistic." Then he seemed to remember what he'd said. And who he'd said it to. "I'm sorry."

"You didn't tell the cops about her."

"No." Gabriel shook his head.

"Do you think she's . . . I mean, it was a really big explosion."

"The Coast Guard is searching the water. And the feds are searching the island. If they find someone—"

"What do you mean if?" April asked.

"We're not going to be the only ones looking for survivors," he said, his eyes a warning.

"You mean the Institute," April said. "So you think they're . . . You think it's . . ."

"It's real," Gabriel said. "All those years, I heard rumors. About a place no one can find. About a veritable army of ghosts. About *an Institute*. I always thought it was some kind of urban legend, but now . . ." He shook his head. "It's real."

It was. April knew in her gut that it was true. Somewhere in the world there was a place where lost children were collected and trained and used. It would have been so easy for April to have been one of them. But they hadn't found her. And she'd found Gabriel.

"Do you think they want me?"

"They can't have you," Gabriel snapped. "You're stuck with me."

April had spent ten years dreaming of a perfect life with her perfect mother, but what she got was this oh-so-imperfect man, and it turned out, the reality was so much better than the dream.

"*Hmmm. Hmmm.* I do hate to interrupt, but breakfast . . . or shall I say . . . brunch is served."

April turned at the sound of the voice. And the smell of bacon. And the sight of the man she hadn't seen in far too long.

"Look who we found!" Colin exclaimed.

"Smithers!"

She ran and threw herself into his arms.

"Hello, Miss April. Am I to understand that I missed quite an adventure during my time away?" Then he saw Gabriel and his sling. "Yes. I see I did."

"Come on. I'll tell you all about it while we eat."

"I will certainly keep a plate hot for you, sir, but I'm afraid you must see to your guest first."

"My guest?" Gabriel didn't look optimistic, but April could see it in his eyes. She could feel it in the pit of her own stomach. "Who?"

"A woman from Child Protective Services arrived a few minutes before you. She was most insistent that she speak with you as soon as you returned. I put her in the library."

Gabriel looked down at April. "Eavesdrop or come with me?"

"Sadie, Tim, and Violet are already on the upper level," Smithers confessed. "But she asked specifically to speak to you, April."

April didn't want to talk to Tiny-Pencil Lady. She wanted to eat all the bacon and take a shower and then watch a million movies. She wanted to be a kid. Just for a little while. A few hours at least.

But she knew it had to be done. She'd been kind of kidnapped. Twice. They might try to take her away again. They might not believe that Gabriel was her uncle. They might not care.

April had to make them care.

So she straightened her filthy clothes and smoothed her windblown hair. She needed to look and act and sound like someone who belonged there.

She needed to be a Winterborne.

So she followed Gabriel to the library doors.

"They might try to take me again," she whispered. Her voice cracked.

But Gabriel sounded as big and strong as Winterborne House itself as he said, "They can try."

And then he pushed open the door to the library and walked toward a woman who most decidedly did *not* have a tiny pencil.

Nope. This woman had a cup of coffee and a plate with tiny scones, and she was looking up at the painting over the fireplace. The fireplace with the secret lock that opened the secret passage that led to the secret lair where Winterbornes had honed their secret legacy for generations.

She was younger than Tiny-Pencil lady. Her clothes were nice but comfortable. The kind you might wear if you were expected to work ten hours a day and never knew where your job might take you.

"Hello. I'm Gabriel Winterborne," Gabriel said. He extended his right hand. His left was in the sling. "I'm so sorry to keep you waiting."

It took her a moment to realize both her hands were full, but then she placed the cup on the mantel and took Gabriel's hand.

A bit of a blush covered her dark cheeks as she looked up at him, windswept and wounded and fresh from saving a little girl. The woman wore a wedding ring, but she had a look on her face that said she was still going to tell everyone in her book club about the time she met a billionaire.

She couldn't possibly have been more different from Tiny-Pencil Lady, and that had to be a good thing. Didn't it?

"Did Smithers give you everything you need, Ms. . . ."

"Jackson. I'm Everly Jackson, Mr. Winterborne. I'll be handling your case. I'm sorry I'm just now getting here."

"That's okay. I just got released from the hospital an hour ago."

"Yes. I heard about that." She looked down at his sling. "You're okay?"

"It's just a scratch." (It was totally more than a scratch.)

"Someone told the officers that April's new guardian was—and I quote—caught in a bloody deep hole, and the police and FBI were going to have to argue about who would get to keep him?"

"That would be Colin."

"April's guardian was named Colin?" Ms. Jackson sounded genuinely confused.

"No. Colin is—" Gabriel pointed overhead, to the four faces that stared down from the balcony. "The one on the right."

Don't do finger guns. Don't do finger guns. Don't—

He totally did finger guns.

"I see," Ms. Jackson said. "Then *who* was April's new guardian?"

This didn't make any sense, but Gabriel was as calm as could be when he said, "Reggie Dupree. I'm sure it's in April's file."

"That's the thing, Mr. Winterborne—"

"Gabriel."

This time she didn't blush. She was all business. "There's nothing in April's file except that she was placed here several months ago. I'm sorry it's taken me so long to get out here. I meant to visit sooner. But we're incredibly understaffed at the moment, and since we knew your accreditation was just a formality, it wasn't our biggest concern, so —"

"You need to talk to the woman with the tiny pencil," April cut in. She didn't want to be rude, but her stomach had been growling for hours, and that was before she knew there were scones *and* bacon waiting in the kitchen.

"Who?" Ms. Jackson asked.

"Gladys Pitts," Gabriel said. "The other agent handling this case."

And then she didn't say anything. Not for a long, long time. April heard everything. The popping of the wood in the fireplace and the creak of the balcony as Tim, Violet, Sadie, and Colin leaned closer so that they wouldn't miss a single word.

But they shouldn't have bothered. Because when the words came, they were as clear as a bell.

"Mr. Winterborne, I'm the *only* agent who has ever

been assigned to this case. And nobody by that name works in our office."

The silence that followed was like a roar inside April's mind.

"Oh." Gabriel turned on his full smile. The fake one that looked like a real one, and only April, Smithers, and the other kids could tell the difference. "My mistake. I must have misunderstood. I'm sorry."

April saw the woman talking with Gabriel. She heard something about paperwork and protocols and formalities that had to be followed. And five minutes later, the stranger smiled and waved at the kids on the balcony and said goodbye. The door opened and closed. And when she was finally gone, April felt the other kids circle round and look at the closed door as if expecting the ghost of Tiny-Pencil Lady to come floating through the heavy wood and scream *boo*.

"So if that's our case agent . . ." Sadie said.

"Who showed up here and handed April over to a murdering lunatic with good taste in candy?" Colin asked.

"That"—Gabriel started, and April felt the déjà vu wash over her like a wave—"is a very good question."

EPILOGUE

It was winter until it was summer. Somehow that year they skipped spring altogether, and one day they woke up to bright sun and clear skies and the sound of Gabriel yelling, "Everybody up! Get up! Get up!"

Maybe it's Izzy! April thought as she rolled out of bed. (It wasn't Izzy.)

Instead, April ran downstairs to find Gabriel wearing shorts and a hat and . . .

"Are those flip-flops?" Colin asked. "I didn't even know he had toes."

"What's going on?" April asked.

"Beach day," Gabriel said. "I thought we'd take the boat to the island."

"Murder Island?" Colin gasped. "No thank you."

"Hey!" Gabriel snapped. "I'm the one who almost died there. Twice. If anyone can call it Murder Island, it's me. And I say it's *Winterborne* Island. But if you don't want to go make a bonfire and eat s'mores . . ."

"Now, let's not be hasty, mate."

They might have argued for hours if Smithers hadn't appeared and said, "Miss April, this just arrived for you."

The envelope was pink, but instead of an address there was just April's name in a loopy handwriting she'd never seen before. She held it for a long time, just staring, because April never got mail and a little part of her couldn't imagine it might be good news.

"Well, you want me to open that?" Colin said, and April took a deep breath, then broke the seal.

"What is it?" Violet stood on her tiptoes, trying to see.

"Ooh! It's a birthday card!" Sadie squealed. "April! I didn't know it was your birthday."

April felt her hands shake. "Neither did I."

"What do you mean? Of course you'd know —"

"Sadie, why don't you guys go put some candles in the picnic basket? We can have birthday s'mores."

"Well, that's not very fair to April. We should have s'mores *and* cake because that's only —"

"Colin!" Gabriel growled.

"And that's our cue," Colin said, grabbing Sadie and Violet and dragging them to the kitchen.

And then it was just Tim. And Gabriel. And April. And a card that felt way too hot in her hands.

"Want me to do it?" Tim sidled closer, but April shook her head.

Then she opened the card and read:

Dear April,

I suppose you still have a lot of questions. I'm afraid I'm just not very good at providing answers. Yet. Maybe someday.

Your father might be locked away, but I'm out of practice on the Mom thing. Or maybe it was just never my forte. Protecting you was my only priority for so long that now it's the only thing I'm good at. So that's what I'm going to do. Forever.

I'm sorry that keeping you safe meant depriving you of a family and a home for so long, but you have both now. You're where you're supposed to be. And me? Well, I'm alive.

Don't let my kid brother get you killed.

Mom.

PS: have a happy birthday.

And for the first time in her life, April did.

CAN YOU SOLVE THE CASE?

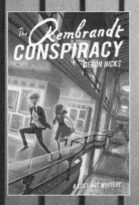

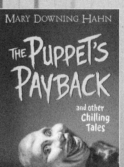